FREDDY
and the FRENCH
FRIES
The Mystery of
Silas Finklebean

D1344140

David Baldacci is a *New York Times* bestselling author of books for adults, such as *Hour Game*, *Absolute Power* and *Split Second*. *The Mystery of Silas Finklebean* is the second book in the Freddy and the French Fries series.

FREDDY and the FRENCH FRIES

The Mystery of Silas Finklebean

David Baldacci

Illustrated by Patrick Harrington

MACMILLAN CHILDREN'S BOOKS

First published 2006 by Little, Brown and Company, USA

First published in Great Britain 2007 by Macmillan Children's Books
a division of Macmillan Publishers Limited
20 New Wharf Road, London N1 9RR
Basingstoke and Oxford
www.panmacmillan.com

Associated companies throughout the world

ISBN: 978-0-330-44919-9

Text copyright © David Baldacci 2007
Illustrations copyright © Patrick Harrington 2007

The right of David Baldacci and Patrick Harrington to be identified as
the author and illustrator of this work has been asserted by them
in accordance with the Copyright, Designs and Patents Act 1988.

1 3 5 7 9 8 6 4 2

A CIP catalogue record for this book is available from
the British Library.

Printed and bound in Great Britain by Mackays of Chatham plc, Kent

To Mrs Doss's and Mrs LeBlanc's
first-grade class,
where Freddy and the French Fries
really came to life

Contents

CHAPTER 1

FRIES DEFINITELY ALIVE

Nine-year-old Freddy Funkhouser and his thirteen-year-old sister, Nancy, were counting up the receipts for the night at their family restaurant, the Burger Castle. As they were finishing, their father, Alfred, walked out from the kitchen, opened a large white umbrella and instantly vanished.

'Omigosh,' said Nancy. 'Now he's really done it. This is worse than him blowing himself up all the time with one of his screwy inventions.'

Suddenly Alfred reappeared, holding the closed umbrella. 'My inventions aren't screwy, dear, just sometimes slightly ahead of their time.'

'Cool, Dad,' said Freddy excitedly. 'You made yourself *invisible*.'

'Not exactly. This umbrella refracts light particles and gives the appearance that the person using it has vanished. Here, try it.'

Freddy opened the umbrella, raised it over his head and disappeared.

'Oh, Dad, if only you could make it permanent,'

said Nancy, looking longingly at the spot where her brother no longer was.

Freddy reappeared and handed the umbrella back to his father. 'Dad, that is, like, *sooo* awesome. Why don't you call it "The Invisibrella"?'

'That's a really cool name, Freddy. I'm working on a bowl that will do the same thing.'

'An Invisi*bowl*?' Nancy said dully.

'Invisibowl. That's a good one too,' Alfred said.

'It certainly has some interesting applications.' He whispered to Freddy, 'But it certainly doesn't top what *you* did.'

Like his father, Freddy was an inventor. And he had invented something – or some*things* – super special that had helped his family recently win a parade float competition against their rivals, the Spanker clan, who owned the enormous Patty Cakes Restaurant across the street.

'Where are they, by the way?' his father asked.

'Hey, guys,' called out Freddy, 'over here.'

The five – or six, if you counted heads – figures came out from the dining area. They were all superpowered French fries that Freddy had built and brought to life with the help of a billion-jiggy-watts lightning bolt. Each Fry was a different colour and didn't look anything like a human, so when they weren't working at the Burger Castle, Freddy had to disguise them with regular clothes, wigs and make-up.

Theodore was an incredibly smart blue crinkle-cut Fry; Ziggy was a tiny yellow Fry; Si and Meese were skinny red shoestring Fries (with one body and two heads); Wally was an enormous purple waffle Fry; and Curly was a green curlicue Fry. The Fries were all disguised as guys except for Wally, who wore a polka-dot dress, a wig and high heels. In the small town of Pookesville, where the Funkhousers lived, he was known as Wilma.

When they were at the Burger Castle, though, the Fries wore no disguises at all. The customers just assumed that the brightly coloured Fries were in costumes because all the Funkhousers wore funny outfits too: Alfred was a tomato, Nancy was a bottle of ketchup and Freddy dressed as a chicken and clucked in greeting to each customer.

'Boy, Mr F,' said a beaming Si, who was always happy. 'That rutabaga meat loaf with a reduction sauce made out of pansies and candle wax with just a dash of that thingamastuff you made in your laboratory was a big seller today. What an aroma. Mm-mm.'

Meese, who was always sad, scowled at his twin and said, 'It smelled like elephant poop and gave me a headache.'

Alfred replied, 'Well, that strong smell halts runny noses on the spot.'

'But we'd sell a lot more of it if you'd just change the name,' said Nancy. 'The "Snot Stop

Special" isn't really all that appetizing when you think about it, Dad,' she added, rolling her eyes.

'That's nice, dear,' said her father absently.

At that instant Howie Kapowie came running into the restaurant waving a piece of paper. Howie was Freddy's only friend – well, his only *human* friend anyway. He was even smaller than Freddy and had rumpled black hair.

'Hey, Freddy, did you see?'

Freddy took the paper and read it while the Fries and Alfred crowded around.

'Wow,' said Freddy. 'A science competition.'

'With a hundred-dollar first prize and your picture in the *Pookesville Tatler* newspaper,' said Howie. He popped three cheese cubes in his mouth and chewed slowly while he fantasized about victory. 'Do you realize how many cheese cubes I could buy with a hundred dollars?'

'Howie,' said Freddy, 'we can work on a project together.'

'That's what I was thinking. I mean, after all, you're the real scientist, but I make a pretty darn good sidekick.'

'Hey,' bellowed Wally. 'Maybe you can invent some food. Not just any food. A mountain of food. No, a whole mountain range of food. No, a whole mountain range of food that keeps growing back even after you eat it.'

As he talked, Wally's eyes grew bigger and bigger and his butt and belly stretched wider and wider.

Freddy gave him a poke and whispered, 'Ixnay on the *purpulis enormosis* thing.' *Purpulis enormosis* was the Latin name that Theodore had christened Wally with because, well, he was purple and enormous. And he, like the other Fries, could morph into virtually anything he wanted to. Nancy watched this spectacle very suspiciously.

While Howie and Alfred already knew what the Fries really were, Nancy was still clueless about their origin. Freddy wanted to keep it that way.

'I hear Adam Spanker's entering the competition,' said Howie.

'In a battle of brains, I'm not afraid of Adam Spanker,' said Freddy confidently.

Adam Spanker headed up a gang that struck fear into the hearts of children all over Pookesville. His father, Stewie Spanker, was the Pookesville police chief, town mayor *and* he owned the Patty Cakes restaurant. It was hard to say who was meaner, the father or the son.

'You never know; he can be tricky,' warned Howie.

'That's good advice,' said Alfred Funkhouser. 'OK, we're heading home, Freddy. Do you want to ride with us?'

'We'll walk home, Dad,' answered Freddy. 'It's sort of a tight fit with Wall – I mean *Wilma* in the station wagon.'

After Nancy and their dad had left, Freddy, Howie and the Fries went into a back room where Freddy took off his chicken costume, and the Fries started to put on their human clothes. Curly pulled several baseballs out of his locker and started tossing them in the air. He entertained the customers at the Burger Castle with his juggling skills and liked to practice whenever he could.

Wally had just put on his high heels and was trying to cram his dress over his head when he stumbled and bumped into Curly.

'Whoops!' said Wally. The collision sent the baseballs Curly had been tossing bouncing down a set of steps leading to the basement. 'Sorry, Curly.'

'That'sokayWallyaccidentshappen,' mumbled Curly. He strung all his words together because Freddy had made a mistake when constructing the green Fry's voice box and hadn't yet figured out how to fix it.

'I'll go get them.' Wally threw his dress on the floor and rushed down the steps and through an open door at the bottom. A second later, they heard a big crash.

'Here we go again,' said Freddy wearily. Yet not even Freddy could imagine how much trouble Wally would be getting them into this time.

CHAPTER 2

THE SPANKER WHAMMO

Freddy got to the basement first. He looked down at the purple blob lying on the floor in front of him. 'Wally, are you OK?'

Wally slowly rose on thick, quivering ankles.

'How do people walk in these itsy-bitsy thingie-wingies?' complained Wally about the ladies' shoes he wore. 'My tootsies are like hamburger.' Wally suddenly got a strange look on his face. 'Hamburger! I am soooo hungry.'

The other Fries caught up.

'Wally,' said Theodore in his deep, scholarly voice, 'you really need to become more proficient in navigating with that particular style of footwear.'

'Theodore,' complained Wally, 'I'm sort of busy trying to figure out how to walk in these dumb shoes, OK?'

'What's that?' squeaked Ziggy, pointing at the spot where Wally had hit the wall.

'Lookslikeaholewithsomethingbehindit,' mumbled Curly, examining the break.

Everyone crowded around Curly, but it was too dark in the hole to see anything.

'I'll go get a flashlight,' Freddy said. Moments later he returned and shone a light in the hole.

'Wow,' exclaimed Wally.

Si said, 'It looks like a passageway. I bet at the end of it there'll be a pot of gold and nothing but good times.'

'I'm sure there're monsters in there just waiting to eat us,' Meese whined. 'Black holes are never good for you. That's why they're dark and scary.'

Freddy peered through the opening. 'There *is* a passageway. I wonder where it goes?'

'Well, the aperture is too diminutive for us to proceed,' opined Theodore.

'Yeah, and the hole's too little to get through,' added Wally, scratching his head.

Theodore looked at the big purple Fry and sighed. 'That's what I just said.'

'Wecouldtrytomaketheholebigger,' mumbled Curly.

'I'm not sure my dad would like that,' cautioned Freddy.

'COMING THROUGH,' roared Wally, who had morphed into a giant purple bowling ball and was rolling right at them.

Freddy and the other Fries jumped out of the

way just in time. Wally hit the wall and broke right through it, disappearing into the darkness.

'Wally!' Theodore cried out as the others peered through the new, very large hole. 'Did you suffer bodily impairment?'

Wally yelled back, 'Nope, but you oughta see the huge boo-boo on my butt.'

Following Freddy, Howie and the Fries cautiously entered the secret passageway.

'Wow,' said Freddy as he shone the light around. 'It looks like something inside a medieval castle in Europe.'

'But the Burger Castle's not very old, is it?' asked Theodore.

'I didn't think so,' said Freddy. 'Before we bought it and turned it into a restaurant, it was a laundromat. I thought those owners had built it, but maybe not.'

They found Wally rubbing his very large behind.

'Are you OK, Wally?' asked Howie.

'I'm cool, little dude. Lucky I didn't hit my head and mess up my big brain.'

'Yeah, lucky,' said Ziggy as they continued down the windy passageway.

Theodore, who, unlike Wally, had two large computer chips for *his* brain, said, 'I calculate that the direction of this tunnel is running north by northeast at precisely forty-five degrees.'

'Wait a minute,' exclaimed Freddy. 'That means it's headed towards the Patty Cakes restaurant.'

Wally rubbed his huge hands together and sniffed the air. 'Yummy. I thought I could smell all that grease frying.'

Ziggy grabbed Freddy's pants leg. 'Uh, Freddy, can we get out of here now? It's sort of, well, spooky down here.'

Wally reached down and picked up the little yellow Fry and put him on his broad shoulders. 'Not to worry, little papoosie, nothing's gonna get you while big Wally's around.'

Just then they heard a loud squeaking noise from the direction they were headed.

'AAAAAHHHHH!'

Freddy was knocked down and lost the flashlight, which went out, plunging them into darkness.

'Ouch!' cried out Ziggy amid lots of scuffling.

Curly mumbled, 'Wouldwhoeveritisplease-getoffme?'

Si said, 'Boy, I've always wondered what it felt like to be smashed to a pulp.'

'We're all going to die, and I'm first in line,' yelped Meese.

Freddy finally found the flashlight and turned it back on.

'Wally!' he said in a scolding tone.

The purple Fry had jumped on top of Howie and the other Fries while still holding Ziggy on his shoulders, causing Ziggy to hit his head on the ceiling.

Wally looked sheepish as he climbed down. 'I went up there for a better look.'

'Come on, guys,' said Freddy. 'We need to see where this passageway goes.'

They cautiously moved along until they reached a doorway.

'Go ahead and open it,' said Si. 'I bet there's a million bucks just waiting on the other side for us to grab.'

'No,' said Meese frantically, 'that's where the monsters are, I'm telling you.'

Theodore was examining the door. 'It appears to be locked.'

Freddy pulled a small device from his pocket.

'Is that a new invention?' asked Howie.

Freddy nodded. 'The Wriggle-Jiggle. It'll take care of that lock.' The Wriggle-Jiggle was a coiled piece of copper wire attached to a small power pack. Freddy put it in the lock, turned on the power, and the wire wound in and around the lock tumblers, pushing them to their open position. They heard a loud *click*, and the door swung open.

'Pretty cool, Freddy,' said Si.

'Thanks. I use it to get into my sister's room and mess things up.'

Carefully making their way through the door, they headed down a short hallway. Here, the passageway seemed to come to a dead end, until Curly pointed up and mumbled, 'Lookslikeatrapdoor-intheceiling.'

Freddy stood on Wally's shoulders and slowly pushed against the door. To his surprise, it opened a few inches. Freddy peered through the crevice and gasped. He was staring directly into the office of Stewie Spanker, the owner of Patty Cakes.

Stewie Spanker was so porky that he could barely fit in the chair behind his enormous desk. He was wearing a pink jumpsuit emblazoned with the Patty Cakes logo and a plastic hat in the shape of a triple-decker hamburger and huge slice of pink cake – and he didn't look very happy.

Then Freddy noticed Stewie wasn't alone. Standing to the side of the desk was Stewie's son, Adam, who looked like a smaller version of his father.

'I still can't believe the Funkies won the float competition,' Adam was saying.

'Don't remind me,' roared Stewie Spanker. 'I spent a ton of money having that float built. And we've lost lots of customers to those wackos. Who in the world would've thought people would actually eat food that was good for them? And *like* it!' He pointed a plump finger at his son. 'Now we have to get back at them for that. You're smart, Adam. You can think of a way, can't you?'

While not a very bright boy, Adam had a

certain talent for coming up with ways to cause trouble. 'I'll think of something, Pop, and when I do' – he smacked a beefy hand into a thick palm – 'Whammo! No more Funkhousers to bug us.'

'I knew I raised you right,' said his father, smiling.

'I'll report back here tomorrow at the same time with my plan,' said Adam. 'Hey, what was that?' he said suddenly, looking around.

Ziggy had sneezed and the sound had carried into the office. Freddy quickly lowered the trapdoor and they all held their breath. A long minute passed and then Freddy eased the trapdoor up a fraction of an inch and peered through.

He saw Adam leaving the office. Breathing a sigh of relief, Freddy lowered the door and got off Wally's shoulders.

'So what'd you hear, Freddio?' asked Si.

Freddy quickly told the gang about the Spankers' scheme.

'So we simply return tomorrow at the same time and we'll discern all the details of his nefarious plan,' said Theodore.

'We can't do that,' said Wally. 'We have to be here listening to the yucky stuff they're going to do to us.'

Ziggy exclaimed, 'That's what he just said, Wally!'

'OK, guys,' said Freddy, 'tomorrow we'll be

back. Once we hear their plan, we'll be ready to beat them at their own game.'

'Uh, Freddy,' said Howie, 'every time we get mixed up with the Spankers, bad things tend to happen. Like, to *us*.'

'Don't worry,' Freddy said confidently as they walked back through the door. 'It'll be different this time.'

But halfway down the hallway Freddy stopped suddenly.

'I don't remember there being another door here,' he said, pointing at a small black door across from them.

Freddy tried the doorknob, but it was locked. He pulled out his Wriggle-Jiggle, yet before he could insert it in the lock, the door swung open.

'YEOW!' said Wally as he jumped on top of Theodore, flattening the blue Fry.

'Ho-how di-did that ha-hap-pen?' Freddy stammered.

There was a flash of light, and the next thing they knew, they were running for their lives. They raced down the hallway, through the hole, into the basement of the Burger Castle, up the steps, out the front doors, across the drawbridge and onto the street.

Stopping to catch his breath, Freddy's mind was whirling so fast he could barely understand what he was thinking. As his head cleared, Freddy was sure of one thing. There had been a man down there, dressed in what looked to be clothes from a very long time ago. He had looked right at Freddy. His mouth was open and he seemed to be trying to say something, but all that came out was one long moan.

And that wasn't all.

The man had lights flashing all around him. And he had been hovering at least two feet OFF the ground!

CHAPTER 3

THEODORE'S COCONUTDUMDUM

At the slightly run-down Funkhouser farm, Freddy, Howie and the Fries dashed into one of the old barns far from the old two-storey house. Freddy pulled a hidden lever and the floor opened under them, and they all fell about ten feet and landed in a soft pile of hay. They were now in Freddy's underground lab.

'I need to fix that,' Freddy reminded himself as he pulled hay out of his navel.

'I wif ud ix it tu,' mumbled Howie, spitting hay out of his mouth.

'Stairs might be in order,' pronounced Theodore as he put back on his glasses.

Wally slowly stood and looked sheepish. 'Uh-oh,' he moaned. Under him was Ziggy, flat as a pancake.

'Sorry, little papoosie,' he said, prying Ziggy off the ground. 'For such a skinny guy, I actually weigh a lot. It must be heavy bones.' As he attempted to help Ziggy up, he accidentally hit the

18

yellow Fry in the back of the head. Ziggy's arms, legs and face immediately fell off.

'I hate when it does that,' cried out Meese. 'It's disgusting to have body parts all over the floor.'

'Boy, I wish my face and arms and legs fell off like that,' declared Si.

'Hey, that's *my* arms and legs you're talking about too,' said Meese. 'And I want them all to stay right where they are.'

Freddy kicked Ziggy in the butt and all Ziggy's parts flew back on. 'I gotta fix that too,' Freddy reminded himself.

The Fries had set up their living quarters in Freddy's lab, and so there were five bunk beds on one side of the wall.

Freddy and the gang all gathered around Freddy's long lab table, which was crammed with equipment and gadgets that he was working on.

'OK, guys, did you see what I saw in the room?' he asked.

They all looked at each other and then at him, and one by one they slowly shook their heads.

Howie explained, 'You were standing in front of me, so I couldn't see anything that was in that room.'

'Yeah, you started screaming and yelling and took off running, so we just followed you,' said Si.

'That'srightIwasscaredbecauseyouwerescared,' mumbled Curly.

'What did you observe that petrified you so comprehensively?' asked Theodore.

'Maybe he should tell us what scared his pants off first, Teddy,' said Wally.

'THAT'S WHAT HE JUST SAID, YOU BIG PURPLE DOUGHBALL,' cried out Ziggy, who was still obviously upset at being smashed flat.

'Well,' said Freddy, 'I saw a man wearing really old clothes. And he was moaning. And that's not all. He was also *floating* in the air.'

The others stared at him dumbfounded, while Theodore scratched his blue chin. 'That is quite a conundrum,' he said.

'I *love* coconutdumdums,' said Wally excitedly. 'With the little marshmallows and whipped cream. Dee-licious.'

'A conundrum,' explained Theodore, 'is a puzzle, a mystery that needs to be solved. It has nothing to do with coconuts, marshmallows or whipped cream, my fine purple friend.'

Wally looked crestfallen. 'Bummer, blue dude.'

They watched as Theodore's eyes spun in his blue head, a sure sign that he was thinking with maximum computing power. At last he said, 'If you saw a man dressed in clothes from a long time ago, and he was floating in the air and moaning, and it wasn't simply a hallucination, then I think you may have been witness to an apparition of supernatural composition.'

'That would've been my guess,' agreed Wally, but then he looked puzzled. 'Uh, what exactly did you just say?'

'I exactly said that I believe Freddy saw a ghost.'

'A GHOST!' screamed Wally, jumping up in the air and hitting his head on the ceiling before falling back to the floor and rubbing his noggin.

Theodore nodded. 'I have just now made a comprehensive evaluation of my databases and that is the only conclusion that conforms to the evidence now available.'

Wally proudly announced, 'I, too, made a com

'. . . a compr . . . uh, a eval . . . er, vul, uh, a . . .' He suddenly smiled and restarted with confidence. 'I made a constipated evacuation of *my* ductwork and that's what I think too.'

Theodore said, 'I think we need to do some research into the actual history of the Burger Castle.'

'Howie and I can go to the town library tomorrow after school,' replied Freddy.

'But Freddy,' said Howie, 'we have to get busy on the science competition. We don't even have a project picked yet.'

'Howie, if Theodore is right and it was a ghost I saw, that would make a terrific science project. If we could discover its source, we could maybe solve one of the greatest mysteries of all time. We'd be a lock to win the competition.'

As Freddy was going to sleep that night, all he could think about was what he'd seen. Had it been a ghost? If so, whose ghost was it? And why was it at the Burger Castle? It was both scary and exciting.

As he finally drifted off to sleep, Freddy hoped tomorrow brought some answers.

CHAPTER 4

THE MYSTERY OF

SILAS FINKLEBEAN

After school the next day, Howie and Freddy rode their bikes to the town library.

'Don't forget, Freddy, we have to register for the science competition as soon as we're done here,' reminded Howie.

Inside the library, they passed a big banner that had been hung across one wall. It read: HAVE A QUESTION? IT'S 'ASK A LIBRARIAN' WEEK.

'Well, I guess we came to the right place for answers,' joked Howie.

At the front desk they asked the elderly librarian for information about the history of Pookesville. She brought out a book, stamped the checkout page, and handed it to Freddy.

'No one's checked out that book in a long time,' she said. 'What are you two boys looking for?' she asked.

'Freddy thought he saw a ghost –' began Howie before Freddy clamped a hand over his mouth and dragged him to a table in a deserted part of the library.

Freddy read the title of the book aloud to Howie. *'The Entire History of Pookesville in 31½ Pages.'*

'Well, it's not that big of a place,' commented Howie.

Freddy flipped through pages and then stopped. 'Omigosh, Howie, look at this picture.'

'That's the Burger Castle!' said Howie excitedly.

'Shhh!'

They both looked up. The librarian had come around the corner and was looking at them very severely. 'This is a library,' she said quietly, 'not a sock hop.'

As she went away, Howie asked, 'Uh, Freddy, what's a sock hop?'

Freddy was reading the story accompanying the picture of the Burger Castle. He said absently, 'I don't know. Must be something only really old grown-ups know about.' He straightened up and turned to his friend. 'Listen to this. I was wrong. The people who owned the laundromat didn't build the Burger Castle building. It was there a long time ago. It says here that the place used to be a private home.'

'Who'd want to live in a place like that?'

Freddy read some more. 'A man named Silas Finklebean, that's who.'

'Silas Finklebean? Never heard of him.'

'Me either, but the book says he was very rich and eccentric. He built the home to remind him of his youth growing up in Scotland. A Scottish castle, I guess.'

'It must have cost a lot of money, even back then.'

'The equivalent of a million dollars in today's money,' said Freddy, reading.

'A million dollars!' Howie cried out.

'Shhh!'

They looked over to see the grey-haired librarian looking at them again. 'This is your last warning. This is a library, *not* a malt shop,' she added shrilly.

As she walked off, Howie said, 'Uh, Freddy, what's –'

Freddy interrupted. 'I don't *know* what a malt shop is either, Howie.' He pointed to a picture of a man dressed in a zebra-striped three-piece suit and a hat and big glasses.

'I guess that's Silas Finklebean, but you can't really see his face with the hat and glasses in the way.'

'Gee,' said Howie, chuckling. 'He sort of dresses like your dad.'

Freddy continued reading the pages. 'It says here that Silas Finklebean was a scientist and inventor. And he made a fortune from one of his inventions.'

'Which one?'

'It doesn't say. Anyway, he used the money from that invention to build the castle.'

'So how did his castle end up being a laundromat and then a restaurant?'

Freddy skipped ahead in the chapter. He read a bit and then his face paled. 'It says here that one stormy night a long time ago, Silas Finklebean went into the basement of the castle. . . .'

'Yeah, yeah,' said Howie. 'And what?'

Freddy turned to face his friend. 'And, he disappeared.'

Howie's big eyes got even bigger. 'When you say "disappeared," what do you mean, exactly?'

'I mean that he disappeared into thin air in the basement of what is now the Burger Castle, and no one knows what happened to him.'

'I really wish you hadn't told me that. Terror makes me wet myself.' Howie paled and crammed five cheese cubes in his mouth.

'After that, the castle sat empty for years. Then someone bought it, but they couldn't live there.'

'UMPHGHEU,' said Howie.

'What?'

Howie swallowed the cheese cubes in one orange lump. 'Why couldn't they live there?' he asked breathlessly.

Freddy read some more. 'Because strange sounds and weird floating things frightened them away.'

'I wish you hadn't told me that. *Utter* terror makes me want to *poop* in my pants.' Howie looked puzzled. 'But, Freddy, how come we've never seen or heard anything like that at the Burger Castle before now?'

'Can I help you with anything?'

They snapped their heads around. There was the librarian again. She sat down and looked at them kindly.

'I'm sorry I was a little abrupt with you earlier. But I have to admit, I *am* curious about why you asked for that book.'

'Do you know anything about a man named Silas Finklebean?' asked Freddy.

She stared at them in surprise for a long moment. Then she said in a low, quiet voice, 'Silas Finklebean? I actually knew him.'

'What!' exclaimed Howie and Freddy together.

'I was a little girl back then, but I remember him as if it were yesterday. People called him the town eccentric, but he was always nice to me. And he helped lots of people in town who needed it. A good Samaritan.'

'So how come they don't have a statue of him in the town square like they do Captain Pookes?' asked Freddy, referring to the soldier who had founded Pookesville.

'Well, I guess they would have, but then he just disappeared.' She added sadly, 'And I guess the people sort of forgot about all the good he'd done for them.'

'Gee, that's not fair,' said Freddy.

'No, it isn't,' she agreed. 'Now, what else can I help you with?'

'We were wondering what Silas Finklebean did to make all that money,' Freddy told her. 'The book says it was from one of his inventions, but it doesn't say which one.'

'Nobody knows which one. And while he was an inventor, I also remember that he was very lucky when it came to betting on things. It seems he never lost.' She paused and looked at them closely. 'Why are you so interested in Silas Finklebean?'

'Well,' said Freddy slowly, 'my dad owns the Burger Castle.'

She clapped her hands. 'I thought I recognized you! You're Freddy Funkhouser. You won the Founder's Day Parade competition.'

'That's right.'

'I'm so glad your family won, because, between you and me, I don't really like the Spankers.'

'They're not easy to love,' said Howie, trying not to laugh.

Freddy asked, 'Uh, do you have a picture of Silas Finklebean? The one in the book doesn't really show his face.'

The librarian got up and returned a minute

later with a small picture. She handed it to them.

'That's Silas Finklebean,' she said quietly.

Freddy's eyes nearly popped out of his head. He grabbed Howie and the book and raced out, leaving the librarian looking stunned.

As they ran down the street, Howie yelled, 'What got into you?'

Freddy looked at him. 'Silas Finklebean was the guy I saw in the Burger Castle basement. The guy *floating* in midair.'

CHAPTER 5

HAROLD J. PUMPERNICKEL

Freddy and Howie ran from the library back to the school, where a long line of students were waiting to enroll in the science competition. As the two boys took a place at the end of the line, someone bumped Freddy hard from behind. He turned to see Adam Spanker standing there with a nasty grin.

'Hey, Funky, don't tell me you're entering the science competition! It's for people with real brains.'

Howie yelled back, 'Freddy has more brains in one of his butt cheeks than you have in your whole body.'

Adam balled up his fists.

'Watch it, Adam,' warned Freddy; 'there're teachers all over the place.'

Adam stuck a big finger in Freddy's chest. 'Yeah, well, there won't always be teachers around, Funky.' He looked past Freddy and his face brightened. 'Hey, Harold.'

A skinny boy with orange hair joined them.

Harold J. Pumpernickel was the only kid in school who might possibly be smarter than Freddy Funkhouser.

'What's happening, Harold?' said Howie.

Harold said shyly, 'Hi, Howie. Hi, Freddy.'

Adam grabbed Harold around the shoulders and pulled him close. 'Hey, no being friends with the enemy.'

'Are you entering the competition, Harold?' asked Freddy.

Adam snapped, '*We're* entering the competition, right, partner?'

'Um, that's right,' answered Harold quietly.

Freddy stared at them, dumbstruck. 'You're partners?'

'Not just partners,' announced Adam gleefully, 'but we're going to win too, aren't we, Harold?'

'I suppose we have as good a chance as anyone,' he said politely.

'Oh, yeah?' said Howie in a confident tone. With all the teachers around he was feeling a lot braver than usual. 'News flash – WE'RE going to win.'

'Ha-ha,' said Adam. 'That'll be the day.'

'We will too win,' insisted Howie.

'Well, if you're so sure, why don't we make a little bet?'

'What kind of bet?' asked Freddy nervously.

Adam said, 'If I win, Funky, you have to come to work at the Patty Cakes for a whole month, without pay, and you have to do everything I tell you to do.'

'And if I win?' said Freddy.

'Not a chance, but then I come to work at the Burger Dump for a whole month.'

'It's the Burger *Castle*,' cried Freddy.

'Whatever. So, is it a deal, Freddy the Freak?' Adam held out a huge hand.

Freddy hesitated, eyeing Adam and then Howie, and finally Harold Pumpernickel.

'What's the matter? Are you scared to bet 'cause you know you're going to lose?' sneered Adam.

'Of course he isn't,' said Howie. 'He's just thinking about what stupid costume he's going to make you wear when we win, right, Freddy?'

Freddy got a stubborn look on his face. 'Right, Howie.' He shook hands with Adam and then yelped as Adam smashed his fingers together in his grip.

'Boy, I can't wait for this contest to happen, Funky. You're going to look really cool in a Patty Cakes uniform taking the garbage out. And without you there to help out, that ratty place you call a restaurant will go out of business.'

Freddy's eyes popped. 'Hey, wait a minute.' Then he suddenly noticed that lots of people in line were listening intently.

'You already shook on it,' said Adam quickly. 'If you try to back out now, everybody will know that you're nothing but stinking, yellow-bellied chicken scum.'

Howie yelled, 'Well, he's not backing out because we're going to beat your tiny brain out.'

'So long, Funky,' crowed Adam, ignoring Howie's taunt. 'We'll get you measured for the Patty Cakes uniform real soon.'

Harold waved feebly to Freddy and Howie and left too.

As they walked off, the crowd around them disappeared. But then Nancy came flouncing by in a pair of fake leopard-skin pants, brown galoshes and a pink scarf that went down to her knees.

'Hey, I heard about your little bet with Adam,' she said.

'Did you come here to back us up?' said Howie eagerly.

'No, I came here to tell you you're going to look pretty stupid in a Patty Cakes uniform.' She blew an imaginary kiss at Freddy. 'There's a sucker born every minute.' And she flounced off.

Freddy yelled after her. 'Hey, the circus doesn't come to town for another month, Nanny Boo-Boo, so you might want to put your clown suit away.' He'd called her Nanny Boo-Boo when he was little, and still did to make her mad.

She turned back around and said in a baby voice, 'Aw, are Fweddy-weddy and Howie-cowie so scaredy-waredy of looking stupid-wupid?'

A bunch of nearby students started howling with laughter.

Freddy turned beet red. 'Just wait, Nanny Boo-Boo, I will too win and then we'll see who looks stupid.' He added under his breath, 'I've got just the thing to take care of you.' But when he looked over at Howie he didn't look very confident.

'What's the matter?' asked Howie.

'What's the matter? What's the matter! If I lose

I have to work at the stupid Patty Cakes and do everything that lunkhead tells me to. For crying out loud, Howie, why'd you say I'd do it?'

'Since when do you listen to me? Besides, you said you weren't afraid of Adam in a competition of brains.'

'He's not the brain I'm worried about. It's Harold.'

'But Harold's not as smart as you.'

'We're actually pretty evenly matched. But don't worry, I'll think of something.' Freddy checked his watch. 'Omigosh, we have to hurry or I'll be late for work at the Burger Castle. And after that we have to sneak into Stewie Spanker's office.'

'But, Freddy, we were pretty lucky they didn't see us last time. How are we going to do that without them spotting us?'

Freddy smiled knowingly. 'I have just the thing, Howie. Come on, let's go.'

CHAPTER 6

NO SPY FRY

Freddy and Howie went to the secret lab under the barn where the Fries were getting ready to go to work. Freddy quickly told them everything they had learned about Silas Finklebean.

'Sounds like an interesting fellow,' said Theodore. 'So the plan tonight is for us to go to the Spankers' lair in time to hear the details of their plot against you.'

'But we were almost caught last time,' said Ziggy.

'That won't be a problem this time,' said Freddy. He pulled out his father's Invisibrella and opened it above his head, instantly disappearing.

'AAGGHH!' screamed Wally. 'Freddy's gone, he's gone!' The purple Fry was so upset he ran straight into a wall and knocked himself out.

Freddy closed the umbrella and reappeared.

'Light particle refraction, undoubtedly,' said Theodore while Curly mumbled, 'WowI'venever-notseensomethinglikethat before.'

'That's right, Theodore,' said Freddy as he and

Curly helped a groggy Wally to his feet.

'The umbrella's big enough to cover me and Howie. And you guys can stay upstairs at the Burger Castle and make sure my Dad and sister don't come into the basement.'

'Your sister never goes in the basement,' said Theodore.

'Well, she might sort of come looking for me,' said Freddy sheepishly.

Theodore eyed him closely. 'Freddy, you didn't do something you shouldn't have, did you?'

'Well, she made me mad so I might have played a teensy-weensy trick on her.'

'Way to go, Freddio,' said Si. 'I'm sure she deserved it.'

'Speak for yourself, you happy-go-lucky maniac,' snapped Meese. 'His sister scares me to death. And if I die, you die!'

After they finished working at the Burger Castle, Freddy and Howie snuck down to the basement with the Invisibrella and a ladder. They had covered up the hole that Wally had made in the wall with an old shelf. They moved it aside and slipped into the secret passageway; soon they reached the trapdoor under Stewie Spanker's office.

Howie took a moment to devour four cheese cubes, swallow and wipe his mouth. 'OK, I'm ready.'

They climbed up the ladder, eased open the trapdoor and peered into the room. It was empty.

'This is perfect, Howie,' said Freddy. 'Come on, hurry.'

They clambered through the trapdoor and stood in a corner. Freddy opened the large Invisibrella over their heads. He was able to confirm their invisibility by looking at a mirror hanging across the room. It didn't show their reflections, but the boys could see each other because the light refraction only took place outside the umbrella.

'Now we just wait and hear their whole plan,' said Howie.

'Shh, someone's coming.'

The door opened and Stewie and Adam Spanker walked through. They looked so ridiculous in their Patty Cakes uniforms that Freddy and Howie had to cover their mouths to keep from laughing. And then it got even worse – or better, depending on how you looked at it.

Stewie Spanker sat down and let out an enormous burp. 'Gotta cut back on those burgers and shakes,' he groaned.

'Ha, that's nothing,' said Adam, and he let out a gigantic fart that seemed to bounce off the walls like cannon fire.

'I knew I raised you right,' said Stewie proudly. 'But grab that can of air freshener and give the room a real good spray, son.'

Freddy and Howie wanted to laugh so hard they could barely breathe. But they also knew the Spankers would tear them apart if they found out they were here.

'OK, son, what have you come up with to get rid of the Funkhousers?'

'An unbelievably brilliant plan that I've already put into place, Dad,' proclaimed Adam proudly.

Howie and Freddy looked at each other and smiled. This was working perfectly.

Back at the Burger Castle, the Fries were cleaning up when Alfred Funkhouser came out of the kitchen.

'Hey, guys,' he said.

'Where is that little monster?' yelled Nancy as she ran out of the broom closet wearing a big hat.

'What's the matter?' asked her father.

'Look at this.' She jerked off the hat and her red hair sprang out. It was a mass of curls and puffed up to about two feet over her head. She looked like walking cotton candy.

Her father remarked in a delicate tone, 'I see you've changed your hairstyle again, dear. It's very, well, it's very interesting.'

'*I* didn't do this,' shrieked Nancy. 'That little jerk did. He must've slipped me one of his stupid perm pills when I wasn't looking.'

Alfred looked very proud. 'A perm pill? What a great idea.'

'Dad! I look like a pink cloud.'

Alfred refocused on his daughter's mass of hair. 'Oh, um, right, dear. I'll tell him that what he did was wrong. Very clever and ingenious, but wrong just the same. Where is Freddy, by the way?'

'Well, he said he was feeling a little under the weather,' said Theodore.

'Yeah, he was puking his guts out the last time I saw him,' added Wally.

Nancy stared suspiciously at who she thought was Wilma. 'I am *so* going to massacre that brat,' she said, still fuming.

'What did you want him for, Mr Funkhouser?' asked Theodore innocently.

'Well, I can't find my Invisibrella and I thought he might have it.'

'Oh, he's got –' began Wally before Ziggy stomped on his toes. 'Ouchie-oochie!' Wally yelled, grabbing his foot.

'I think what Wilma was saying,' explained Theodore, 'was that if Freddy had *gotten* it, we would have seen it. And we didn't.'

'OK,' said Alfred, looking a little confused. 'Well, I'm sure it's around here somewhere. I need to find it and work out some bugs.'

'Bugs?' said Theodore quickly.

'I love bugs,' replied Si. 'Bugs are my friends.'

'Good, because you sure don't have any others,' said Meese.

'But you're my friend,' said Si, looking hurt.

'I'm attached to you at the hip. That doesn't make us buds.'

'Uh, exactly what sort of bugs?' asked Theodore.

Alfred said, 'The last time I tried it, I became visible after about three minutes, and then streams of light started shooting out of the umbrella. Probably a loose wire.'

The Fries looked at each other in panic.

'UhboyIthinkwebettergoyouknowwherelikeyouknowveryfast,' mumbled Curly.

'What did he say?' asked Alfred.

'He said we have to leave the premises in the most expeditious manner possible,' said Theodore.

'No, he didn't, he said RUN!' yelled Wally, who blew past them down the stairs to the basement.

The rest of the Fries took off after him, leaving Alfred and Nancy behind.

Once her father left to continue his search, Nancy looked in the direction where the Fries had run. She glanced back to make sure her father was gone and then she raced off after the Fries.

CHAPTER 7

CURLY TO THE RESCUE

'OK, Dad,' crowed Adam to his father, 'here's the deal. I suckered Harold J. Pumpernickel into helping me on the science fair competition.'

'Pumpernickel?' said his father, outraged. 'His father's a garbage truck driver. I don't want you associating with people like that.'

'I know, I know, but the little twerp's got brains – enough brains to take down Freddy Freako. And even better, I got that idiot Funkhouser to bet on the competition.'

Under the Invisibrella, Freddy balled up his fists at this insult.

'Our science project is going to be a huge volcano that we're going to build in the vacant lot next to the Patty Cakes,' proclaimed Adam proudly.

'A volcano!' exclaimed Stewie Spanker.

'Yep. A volcano. Harold says he can make it work just like the real thing, only when it erupts it'll be some goopy stuff coming out instead of lava.'

Stewie jumped out of his chair. 'Erupts! But it'll hit the Patty Cakes.'

Adam laughed. 'Nope, that's the brilliant part. Harold can make the goop go in any direction he wants with some thingamajig he's putting in. So it'll cream the *Burger Dump* instead. It gets covered with four feet of sticky goop and they're out of business. On top of that, I win the competition, and Funky has to come work at the Patty Cakes for a month, where I can make his life miserable.'

'But the Pumpernickels are honest people with integrity, so Harold might tell somebody the truth – the dirty, stinking *rat*.'

'He doesn't know about my plan. I'm going to sneak in when the volcano's finished and aim it at the Burger Dump, and then I'll blame it all on Harold because he'll be doing all the work on it. See, it's perfect.'

His father stared at him for a long moment and then said, 'That is the most dirty, underhanded, despicable plan I've ever heard.' He paused and wiped away a tear. 'I love it, son.'

Freddy was getting madder and madder as he listened. Then he felt something poking him on the shoulder. It was Howie; he was pointing across the room.

Freddy didn't understand what the big deal was. All he could see was himself and Howie in the reflection of the mirror.

Freddy's eyes popped. THEIR REFLECTION!

If the Spankers simply looked in their direction, they were dead. Freddy and Howie stood as quietly as they could and held their breath.

Then something even worse happened. The Invisibrella started turning different colours. The Spankers would see that any second. Howie gulped and started to put a cheese cube in his mouth.

Freddy caught his breath as something grabbed him and lifted him off the floor. The Invisibrella fell, but before it hit the floor it was snatched up too. Freddy and Howie were yanked across the room and through the trapdoor, which slammed shut behind them. 'What was that?' yelled Adam Spanker, looking around the room suspiciously. He walked over to where Freddy and Howie had been standing and looked around. Then on the floor he saw something and picked it up. It was Howie's cheese cube. Adam started thinking hard – at least hard for *him* – and then smiled wickedly.

Down in the underground passageway Curly put Howie and Freddy down after using his long arms to zip them to safety.

'Wow, Curly, you saved our butts,' said a breathless Freddy.

'Yeah, I thought we were goners for sure,' added Howie.

'GladIcouldhelp,' mumbled Curly.

Theodore quickly told the boys about the Invisibrella's bugs.

'Figures. My Dad always has lots of bugs to work out. But it was worth it, because now I know Spanker's entire plan. Come on, let's get out of here.'

They ran back down the passageway, turned a corner and ran smack into Nancy, her hair wrapped in a black scarf. She undid the scarf and her wild hair shot out. 'Look familiar?' she snapped.

Freddy had to cough back a laugh. 'Why, Nanny Boo-Boo, I've never seen you look so beautiful.'

'Don't ever fall asleep, Freddy Funkhouser, or you might wake up with no hair at all. Or no *head*, even.'

'You don't scare me.'

She grabbed the Invisibrella out of Curly's hands. 'Wait'll I tell Dad you were using his stuff.' She stopped and demanded, 'OK, I want to know exactly what you and your gang of freaks have been doing down here.'

'I don't have to tell you anything,' answered Freddy hotly.

'Fine, then you can tell Dad after I tell on you.'

Si stepped forward, 'Hey, kiddo, we don't have to do anything hasty like that. What say we just keep it on the QT?'

Nancy stared at him with contempt. 'Look, you double-headed dum-dum, I'm not keeping anything on the QT.'

Theodore said in a gracious voice, 'Young lady, it's easy to see that you are a person of uncommon intelligence and wit, with a strong sense of style and theatricality.'

'Well, at least one of you has taste,' she said, glaring at Freddy.

'I believe Freddy wanted to keep this a secret because he didn't want to spoil the surprise.'

'Surprise, what surprise?' she said.

'Yeah, what surprise?' said Freddy before Theodore kicked him in the shin.

Theodore continued, 'Quite by accident we stumbled upon this secret area and Freddy thought what a wonderful idea it would be to turn it into an extension of the Burger Castle. We could have seating down here, little rides for the children, perhaps a haunted mansion area with thrills and scary things popping out and a *stage* where plays could be produced.'

'A stage! For plays!' said Nancy. 'I don't believe it!'

'It's quite true,' said Theodore. 'And Freddy was just now saying that it would be perfect for someone with your talents to oversee such an operation, including perhaps acting in several of the productions. Despite what you might think, he is very well aware of your talent as an actress.' Theodore added diplomatically, 'He's told us many times exactly what he thinks of you.'

Nancy stared at Freddy in disbelief. 'Really?'

'Absolutely,' said Theodore. 'In fact, we're in the process of drawing up the plans to build it. I think you'll be very pleased with the result.'

Nancy gave her brother a hug and then started bawling all over his shirt. 'Freddy, that's the most wonderful thing anyone's ever done for me. I even forgive you for what you did to my hair. I don't know what to say, you adorable little cutie-pie,' she gushed between sobs.

'Yeah, me either,' Freddy said, shooting a nasty look at Theodore.

'I won't let you down, Freddy,' she said. 'I'm going to go and start writing up some scripts and picking out some costumes. Oh, I've got so much to do.' She hurried away.

Freddy said, 'Thanks, Theodore; that was actually a pretty good idea. Until she finds out it's all a lie, and then I'm dead.'

'Sorry, Freddy, it's the best I could do at the moment.'

'Well, let's get back to the lab and start planning how we're going to turn the tables on Adam.'

They headed back down the passageway, and then Freddy stopped dead. There was the door again that led to the room where he had seen Silas Finklebean floating in the air. And the door was wide open.

'Uh, guys,' he began.

'Don't even think it, Freddy,' squeaked Ziggy.

'But I saw Silas Finklebean in that room. I don't know if he was a ghost or not, but he was there.' Freddy looked at Theodore. 'What do you think?'

'I think that there's something behind that door that needs to be investigated.'

Freddy drew a deep breath. 'OK, everybody, let's go.' They all started forward except Wally, who wasn't moving. They looked back at him.

The purple Fry said sheepishly, 'So when you said everybody you meant, like, everybody?'

'MOVE IT, PURPLE BUTT,' shouted Ziggy, and Wally shot into the room.

The others quickly followed, and the door slammed shut behind them.

CHAPTER 8

THE FINKLEBEAN SPECIAL

Freddy and the gang jumped when the door closed behind them. Meese tried to yank it open. It wouldn't budge, and he started bawling. 'We're going to die! The ghost of Silas Finklebean is coming to get us.'

Meanwhile, Freddy had been looking around at the room. 'Wow,' he exclaimed. 'This must be Silas Finklebean's secret laboratory.'

The dusty place was filled with funny-shaped bottles containing lots of different-coloured liquids. In one corner was a long table with electrical wires attached to it that looked like something out of a Frankenstein movie. In another corner was a car, but all its wheels were curved and pointed to the right.

'Freddy,' called out Theodore, who was examining a large, leather-bound book on one of the tables. 'Come and look at this.'

They all crowded around the book. The handwriting and diagrams on the pages were neat and clear.

'This must be a log of Finklebean's inventions,' said Freddy excitedly. 'See, there's his name right there.' He pointed to the inside cover of the book.

Wally picked up a bottle filled with a bright blue liquid off the table and sniffed it.

'Wally,' said Theodore sharply, 'Don't drink that. You don't know what it is.'

Wally sniffed it again. 'Not so bad. A combination of mold, lice, and stale fish with just a pinch of body odor.' He took a sip and smacked his lips. 'I've had worse.'

'Wally, that is gross!' Ziggy exclaimed, horrified.

'IthinkI'mgoingtobesick,' said Curly, who was indeed looking a little greener than usual.

Suddenly Wally grabbed his stomach.

'What's the matter, Wally?' asked Ziggy. 'You look like you're gonna puke.'

Wally went from purple to green to blue and then back to purple. 'No, I think I'm OK –'

But suddenly, fast as a purple wind, Wally shot to the ceiling, bounced off, blasted over to one wall, hit it and then went zooming across the room to the other side. Everyone dropped to the floor as he rocketed by overhead.

'Wally, can't you stop?' said Freddy.

'I'm trying, little dude,' Wally yelled back, 'But it's not working.'

Finally, after whizzing around the room for

several minutes, Wally finally dropped out of the air and landed with a thud and didn't move. They all raced over to him.

'Is he dead?' asked Ziggy. 'I think he's dead.'

'He's not dead,' answered Freddy. 'He's just playing dead. Right, Wally?'

Thankfully, Wally slowly sat up.

'I wonder what that stuff was,' said Freddy, eyeing the bottle.

'I don't know,' said Wally. 'But could I have another little sip?'

'NO!!' Freddy and Ziggy shouted together.

'YEOW!!'

They all turned and saw Si and Meese in the car with the curved wheels. They had somehow started it and were now flying around in circles.

'Let me outta here,' screamed Meese.

Si was driving and looked extremely pleased. 'Boy, this baby has some get-up-and-go even if we're not actually *going* anywhere.'

Meese finally managed to hit a stop button. When they got out, they were so dizzy that they immediately fell over.

Theodore held up the logbook. 'That particular device is listed in here as the "Spinner-Winner." Finklebean noted that it had no practical application because one couldn't actually get anywhere in it.'

'Candy,' shouted Wally suddenly. He picked up

a single candy bar that had been under an-other
cover. He quickly devoured it in one bite, but one
crumb of candy fell to the floor. This tiny piece
instantly grew it into another candy bar.

Wally's eyes nearly popped out of his head, and
then he looked like he might cry from sheer joy.
He ate the second bar, leaving a little crumb
behind. It grew into another bar that he ate too. In
the space of ten seconds, he did this a dozen times.
'I'm so happy,' he said.

'The Hydra Chocolate Bar,' read Theodore
from the logbook. 'Billed as the only candy bar
you'll ever need. However, there wasn't much profit
in selling only *one* to each customer.'

'Geez,' said Freddy, 'all I've seen are stupid inventions that couldn't possibly make any money.'

'Well, there is *this*,' said Theodore, pointing to some complicated plans in the logbook. 'I don't see a corresponding invention here for these drawings.'

Freddy looked at them. 'I wonder what it does?'

'It doesn't say, which is curious, because all of the other plans are meticulously labelled,' replied Theodore.

Freddy snapped his fingers. 'I know, we can ask my Dad. Maybe he'll be able to tell what it is.'

'But, Freddy,' cried Si. 'Remember, the door won't open.'

'I'll try the Wriggle-Jiggle.'

But, as they were standing there, the door opened all by itself.

Wally was the first through the door. The others dashed after him before the door shut again. As they disappeared down the hallway, something seemed to be watching them go.

CHAPTER 9

SOME FUNKY ANSWERS

When the gang left the Burger Castle, they were stunned to see that construction of the volcano in the empty lot across the street had started. They stood and watched as Harold, using a remote-controlled robotic arm, built a giant frame of wooden boards.

'Wow, that's pretty cool, Harold,' called out Freddy across the street.

Harold turned around and smiled. 'Hey, thanks, Freddy.'

Suddenly Adam popped up from a lounge chair. He had a super large milkshake in one hand and a huge hamburger in the other. 'Hey, no talking to the enemy, Pumpernickel,' he yelled.

Harold looked afraid. 'I'm sorry, Adam.'

'Hey, hey, what did we talk about, Pumperhead?' demanded Adam.

'Um, I mean, *Captain* Spanker,' Harold said, glancing nervously at Freddy.

'You wanna give up right now, Freako?' said Adam with a loud snort. 'Because you're not going to be able to beat the volcano.'

'Oh, yeah, you just wait and see what we're building,' called out Si.

'Yeahjustwaitandsee.Uhwhatexactlyarewe-building, Freddy?' mumbled Curly.

'Atta boy, Curly, you tell him,' called out Si, slapping the green Fry on the back. 'Even though I have no idea what you just said, I'm sure it was kick-butt stuff.'

'You dopes don't have a clue. You're all losers,' said Adam nastily.

'Just give me the word and I'll eat Adam for you, Freddy,' said Wally. 'Even if he'll give me really bad gas.'

'The best thing we can do,' said Freddy, 'is beat him in the competition.' He held up the logbook. 'Come on, let's go see my dad.'

Alfred Funkhouser was inside the farmhouse working on something when Freddy and the gang arrived.

Alfred pointed at the old logbook Freddy was carrying. 'What's that, son?'

Freddy quickly showed the plans to his father, who started rubbing his chin with his hand, a sure sign his brain was in super-thinking mode.

'Where did you get these plans, Freddy?' he asked, looking at the name 'Silas Finklebean' on the logbook's cover.

Freddy was ready for this. 'It was the librarian in town. She knew Silas Finklebean when she was very young. She found this book on the shelf. He must have donated it or something.'

'That's funny, because it doesn't have a library card on the back page,' said his father.

Thinking quickly, Freddy said, 'Well, it must have come from some special collection. She said no one had ever checked it out before.'

'I see,' said Alfred Funkhouser.

'So what's your considered opinion, Mr Funkhouser?' asked Theodore.

'Yeah, Mr F, let's have the quick down-and-dirty from that big old noggin of yours,' said Si.

'Well, judging from the drawings and the notations at the bottom of each page, which include standard descriptions of quantum theory, black holes, wormholes and string theory that serve as the very backbone of the interconnectedness of the entire universe –'

'Me love worms!' shouted Wally.

Alfred smiled. 'They're not those sorts of

worms Anyway, Freddy, to answer your question, I'd say this was a time travel machine.'

'Time travel machine!' exclaimed Freddy.

'Yes. But it's very curious. The dates in this book are from long ago. Mr Finklebean must have been a man very much ahead of his time. String theory, for instance, is a fairly recent discovery. I can't believe I've never heard of him. Who is he?'

'Just some guy,' said Freddy mysteriously.

'Well, he was obviously very brilliant.'

Freddy took back the logbook.

'What are you going to do with it, Freddy?' asked his father.

'Oh, nothing.' But under his breath Freddy muttered, 'I'm going to beat a volcano, that's what.'

CHAPTER 10

THE STAR OF NANCY

The next night after the restaurant closed, Alfred Funkhouser was putting on his jacket when Nancy walked up. He did a double take because his daughter was dressed in a long gown, pink flamingo sunglasses and a tiara.

'Father, have you seen my darling little brother, Frederick?' she said in a perfect British accent.

He looked at her, stunned. 'Frederick? Uh, are you feeling OK, dear?'

'Fine, why?'

'Well, I've never heard you call Freddy anything, well, anything really *nice* before.'

'Father,' she said haughtily, 'whatever do you mean? I've always held my dear sibling in the highest regard.'

'I see. Um, that costume . . . ?' He looked pointedly at her outfit.

'Well, now that I'm a Broadway star, Father, I must dress the part, mustn't I?'

'A Broadway –'

Nancy interrupted. 'So do you know where Frederick is?'

'I think he went into the basement to do something.'

Nancy strutted off, taking imaginary bows to imaginary audiences. Alfred shook his head. He did that a lot with his two rather unique children.

Freddy, the Fries and Howie were standing inside Finklebean's secret lab.

'OK, guys,' said Freddy, 'Here's the list of items in the plans that we'll need to build the time travel machine, plus some others that I came up with. We'll take anything useful that we find here.' He eyed Wally. 'Just don't drink or eat anything.'

'Right, Freddy,' said Wally. But behind his back the purple Fry crossed his fingers.

The Fries fanned out. All at once they started pulling off covers and looking in drawers and up on shelves for the items on the list. But after a half hour they had only assembled a few pieces.

Freddy looked at the small pile. 'Well, we'll just have to get the stuff we need from some other place.'

Theodore was also looking at the plans. 'That might be a long list,' he said.

'Yeah, Freddy,' said Howie, 'and we have to get going on the science project or else you'll lose the bet and have to wear that stupid Patty Cakes uniform.'

Freddy looked at his friend in exasperation. 'Howie, don't you get it? The time travel machine *is* our science experiment.'

Howie's jaw dropped at this news, and then he snapped, 'I knew that. What, you think I'm stupid or something?' He stuffed three cheese cubes in his mouth and chomped on them in a huff.

They gathered up everything they had collected and left the lab. On the way back down the passageway they ran into Nancy in her crazy costume.

'Oh, Frederick,' said Nancy in her exagger-ated British accent, 'I simply must speak with you about the theatre project.'

'Theatre project?'

'Yes, you know, the one you're building down here for me.'

Theodore pinched Freddy on the arm. 'Oh, theatre, right,' said Freddy.

'I was thinking that right over here would be a simply wonderful place for the marquee,' she said, pointing to one of the walls. 'My name, of course, will be in lights. Nothing *too* large. I am a *modest* superstar after all. I'm thinking just three- or four-foot-high letters.'

'Three or four feet!' cried Freddy.

Nancy put her arm around her little brother. 'Now, we need to talk about my dressing room. I want a very large star on the door, of course, and then a small kitchen and a fireplace and lots of closet space. And a telephone. For all those major interviews,' she said. 'And also the press confer-ences and the occasional meeting with some incredibly lucky member of my fan club. And a salon, where I can entertain after the show. Nothing too grand, only enough to hold a few dozen people.'

'A few dozen!' said Freddy, his eyes bulging.

'I've drawn up some sketches for what I think the Nancy S. Funkhouser Imperial Theatre and

Museum should look like.' She handed him a thick sheaf of rolled-up papers.

'Theatre *and* museum?' asked Freddy. 'What museum?'

'Well, my public will want a place where they can see costumes I've worn in various award-winning plays, as well as signed copies of my marvellous scripts. We can sell T-shirts, baseball caps, coffee mugs and assorted other memorabilia, all with my picture on them, of course. I have an entire marketing campaign put together to ensure that the Nancy S. Funkhouser Imperial Theatre and Museum will be the world's most popular vacation destination.' She snorted. 'Disney World will be a distant second.'

Freddy wanted to say something – actually, he wanted to scream – but nothing would come out.

'Frederick, I can see that you're positively speechless about my grand ideas, and who can blame you, you adorable little unimportant person who's attached himself to my star coat-tails.' She pinched his cheeks. 'Well, I must go. I have millions of things to do. Ta-ta.' She blew them all kisses and swept away.

Freddy finally looked over at Theodore, who smiled weakly.

'Well, you must admit, Freddy, the young lady does have a vivid imagination,' commented Theodore.

'She's a total nutcase!' cried Freddy. 'OK, let's go, guys,' he said miserably. 'We have a science competition to win.'

CHAPTER 11

THE SCIENCE OF COMPETITION

When the gang got outside, Freddy stopped abruptly and the others bumped into him.

'What's up, Freddio?' asked Si.

Freddy pointed across the street. In front of the Patty Cakes restaurant sat a dilapidated old station wagon and next to it an even more beat-up trash truck.

'I think that's Harold's dad's truck,' said Freddy. 'And that's his mom's station wagon.'

As they watched, Harold's entire family came out of the restaurant. Harold had four brothers and sisters. They were carrying big boxes filled with burgers, fries, cakes and pies and other food. They crammed the boxes inside the station wagon and the cab of the truck. Freddy glanced over at the volcano and saw that Harold was still working on it. Harold turned and waved to his family, who waved back at him.

'Come on, son,' said Harold's father. 'It's time to go home.'

Right then, Adam Spanker and his father appeared at the door of the Patty Cakes. Freddy and the gang hid behind some bushes and continued to watch.

'He's got some more work to do,' said Stewie Spanker. 'We'll drive him home in the Cadillac.' He looked at the Pumpernickel's old cars in disgust. 'I'm sure he'd like that a lot better.'

'But it's late,' said Mrs Pumpernickel, 'and he still has to do his homework.'

'He's a smart kid. He can do it fast,' said Adam with a snarl.

'And remember,' said Stewie Spanker, 'You should be grateful we're giving you all that food.'

'We are, we are,' said Mrs Pumpernickel quickly, although her husband didn't look very happy about it. He was a very big man with thick orange hair like Harold's, and he wore blue overalls and heavy work gloves.

'I want Harold home in one hour,' Mr Pumpernickel said. 'No later.' He stared down at Stewie Spanker. Then he glanced up at his son on the volcano's frame. 'Harold, you be careful up there, son, OK?'

'OK, Dad.'

The Pumpernickels got in their vehicles and drove off. The Spankers immediately rushed over to Harold.

'OK, listen up, pumpkin head,' said Adam. 'We're running behind schedule, so you better start working harder.'

'I'm working as hard as I can, Adam.'

'Hey, hey, what are you forgetting?'

Harold sighed. 'I mean, Captain Spanker.'

'You don't want Freddy Freako to win, do you?' snapped Adam.

'I think the person with the best project should win. That's what's fair.'

Stewie Spanker roared, 'Fair has nothing to do with it. Winning is everything. And don't you forget it, you little twerp.' He turned and stomped away.

Adam scowled at Harold. 'So you just better do what you're told or there'll be no more food for your family. Got it?' Then he stormed off, leaving behind a very depressed Harold.

Freddy and the gang had heard all of this.

Theodore rubbed his chin like Alfred Funkhouser did when he was thinking hard. 'So that's why Harold is working with Adam. His family needed food.'

Freddy looked crestfallen. 'I didn't know they were that bad off. We would have given them any food they needed.' Freddy stared over at Harold working all alone on the big volcano, and he got a very determined look on his face. 'Come on, guys, we're going to help Harold.'

'Are you nuts?' cried Howie. 'We're in a competition, Freddy. We can't help them win. Heck, we haven't even *started* our project.'

'There are some things more important than winning,' said Freddy.

'Good grief,' complained Howie. 'What kind of thinking is that?'

Theodore smiled. 'I believe one might call it the beginning of wisdom.'

They trooped over to Harold and told him what they'd come to do.

He was overwhelmed. 'But, Freddy, I don't know what to say.'

'The only thing you have to say, Harold, is what you want us to do,' replied a smiling Freddy.

The gang started working alongside Harold. While Harold wasn't looking, Curly used his long arms to bring boards and rolls of chicken wire up onto the wooden frame, where Ziggy would nail them in under Harold's direction. They mixed up the goop that would be used to cover the frame and chicken wire to make it look like a volcano. Very soon, they had Harold way ahead of schedule.

As they climbed down from the volcano, Harold said, 'Thanks, Freddy. I don't know what I'd have done without your help.'

'It's OK, Harold. That's what friends are for.'

Harold looked embarrassed and was about to say something when they all heard a familiar voice.

'Hey, pumpkin head, what have I told you about talking to the enemy,' yelled Adam Spanker as he came running out of the Patty Cakes.

'They're not the enemy, they're my friends,' said Harold hotly.

'They're spies, you little dope.'

Freddy faced Adam. 'He needed help and we helped him. And you're his partner, so why aren't *you* helping him?'

Adam balled up his fat fists. 'You wanna get knocked into next week, nerd?'

The Fries all stood behind Freddy. 'I think you're outnumbered,' said Freddy.

Adam laughed, ran over to his lounge chair, and pulled out his paintball gun from behind it. He pointed it at the gang. 'OK, who wants to get blasted first?'

Things were looking ugly when a calm voice said, 'Boys, I think it's time everyone went home.'

They turned and there was Alfred Funkhouser. He walked over to them. 'Hello, Harold,' he said. 'How's your family doing?'

'Fine, Mr Funkhouser. Uh, Freddy and his friends were just helping me.'

'Actually, I saw them,' said Alfred, with a smile. 'Come on, Harold, you can drive home with us.'

'But he's *my* partner,' yelled Adam. 'And my dad's driving him home.'

'That's right!' roared Stewie Spanker, who had just raced outside. 'In my brand new Cadillac over there.'

They all looked over to see Wally sniffing around the car.

'Me smell something really good,' he moaned.

'Hey, get away from my car,' yelled Stewie.

'There's food in there,' said Wally.

'You bet there is, you big polka-dotted freak. There's a box of our special super fatted barbecue ribs that I'm taking home for my midnight snack. Now get away from there.'

Wally was drooling all over the Cadillac. 'Me love barbecue.'

'OK, you asked for it,' yelled Adam. He pointed his paintball gun at Wally's big butt and fired.

'Look out, Wal–, er, I mean, Wilma!' yelled Freddy.

At that instant Wally bent through the driver's side window to get to the barbecue, and the paintball bullet hit the windshield and splattered it in black paint.

'AAAAHHHH!' screamed Stewie. 'My beautiful car!'

'Well,' said Alfred Funkhouser, 'I guess you won't be driving Harold home now.'

Stewie didn't answer. He was too busy trying to get the barbecue ribs away from Wally. And losing.

CHAPTER 12

LYDIA THE LUNATIC

The Funkhousers had a very nice visit with the Pumpernickels. Harold told his family how Freddy and his friends had helped him, and Mrs Pumpernickel was so grateful that she went into the kitchen and made them some cupcakes from her special recipe.

Alfred Funkhouser proclaimed them the best he had ever tasted. The Fries had to stop Wally from eating them all.

'Please,' he moaned, 'I just want a few hundred more.' The Pumpernickels chuckled at the very odd-looking woman in a polka-dot dress with big red hair.

Alfred Funkhouser spent quite a bit of time talking with Mr and Mrs Pumpernickel. After they left, Freddy asked his dad what they were talking about, but Alfred just smiled.

The next day after school Freddy and the gang all met at Freddy's lab. After looking over the plans and checking the things they had gotten from Silas Finklebean's laboratory, Freddy studied a checklist he and Theodore had prepared.

'OK, here are the things we still need for the time travel machine.' He split the list in two and handed half to Si and said, 'You, Meese and Curly try to get these things.' He handed the other half to Ziggy and said, 'You and Wally see if you can get these things.'

The Fries studied the list.

'Uh, Freddy,' squeaked Ziggy, 'where do we get this stuff?'

'Try the hardware store. And Si and Meese and Curly can go to the junkyard that's over by edge of town. Just do the best you can. Theodore, Howie and I will stay here and get to work.'

'Sounds like an excellent stratagem for ultimate success, Freddy,' commented Theodore.

'Yeah, and what you came up with might just work too, Freddio,' added Wally.

Twenty minutes later, Ziggy and Wally entered the hardware store. They were both dressed in their disguises. The store clerk behind the counter stared at Wally. The purple Fry's large size would have made him stand out anyway. But in his polka-dot dress, red wig and high heels, he was impossible to miss.

The man's gaze went from Wally to tiny Ziggy,

whose black hair styled in a bouncy pompadour was in sharp contrast to his very pale skin. His jeans, plaid shirt and tennis shoes – though the smallest Freddy could find – were too big for him, so he looked even smaller than he actually was.

'Are you a midget?' the store clerk asked Ziggy.

'No, I'm ZIGGY!' He yelled the last word so loud the air blowing out of his mouth knocked the store clerk's toupee off, and it flew into Wally's mouth.

Wally swallowed and then gagged. 'Hairball,' he croaked. The clerk had not noticed that his hair was missing. He just stared, dazed, at Ziggy.

Ziggy looked embarrassed, cleared his throat and said in a squeaky voice, 'Sorry about that.' He pulled out the list Freddy had given him while Wally stared at shelves filled with absolutely nothing that was edible, though that never stopped the purple Fry.

'What cool stuff!' Wally said, his tongue hanging out at the dozens of cans of paint on the shelves.

'Here's what we need,' said Ziggy, handing the clerk the list. The clerk was now staring at Wally.

'Hey, didn't I see you on TV?' asked the clerk.

Wally spun around and looked very happy. 'Me, on TV?' He batted the long, fake eyelashes that were part of his disguise.

'Yeah, you're one of those professional lady wrestlers, right?' He snapped his fingers. 'Now I remember, you're Lydia the Lunatic. You know, you come out tied up in a straitjacket with drool coming out of your mouth.'

'I'm a good drooler,' said Wally. 'Ask anybody.'

Ziggy said, 'Uh, we're really in a hurry, mister.'

The man studied the list and then his mouth gaped. 'Titanium beams! Glass that'll withstand three thousand degrees! Four thousand rivets!'

'And don't forget the last item,' Ziggy pointed out.

'I can't read it,' said the clerk. He pointed it out to Ziggy.

'That's a nuclear reactor turbine,' answered the yellow Fry. 'Do you have different-sized ones? I think we'll need a pretty big one.'

'A REALLY BIG ONE,' said Wally, who had opened a can of blue paint and was sniffing it. 'And do you have one in purple? That's my favorite colour of all time.'

'A nuclear reactor turbine! That's a joke, right?' said the clerk.

'Freddy didn't say that a nuclear reactor turbine was a joke, did he, Wally?' asked a confused Ziggy, who had no idea what a nuclear reactor turbine was.

Wally was licking the paint with his big tongue. 'No, but he didn't say it wasn't a joke either.'

'That's a good point,' said Ziggy as he looked back at the clerk. 'OK, you can give us a joke nuclear reactor turbine if you have one in stock.

But we don't have time to order one. So whatever you have that's close will be just fine.'

'And don't forget, we want a purple one,' added Wally, who had tipped the paint can to his mouth and was now drinking it.

'Hey,' exclaimed the clerk, 'You can't do that.'

Wally swallowed and wiped his blue mouth, instantly turning his hand blue too. He belched and then looked embarrassed. 'Sorry, blueberries always do that to me. You wouldn't happen to have something in a grapefruit, would you? That keeps me regular.'

The clerk looked at them both. 'Nuclear reactor turbines! Blueberry paint! You two are nuts.'

'Actually, we're Fries, but that's a whole other story,' said Wally, who then caught himself. 'Whoops, I'm pretty darn sure I wasn't supposed to tell you that.'

'Get out of here before I call the cops.' The clerk grabbed the can that Wally was holding and tugged on it.

'Give me that!' cried out the clerk.

'OK,' said Wally, who immediately let go. The clerk went flying backwards, and the can of paint landed on his head. As he pulled it off, he discovered his toupee was gone. He yelled frantically, 'Where's my hair?'

Wally burped, and something flew out of his mouth and he caught it. He handed it to the clerk. It was the toupee – which was now blue too. 'It'll go very nicely with your new colouring,' Wally said.

When the clerk saw his hair he jumped up, grabbed a broom and started charging them.

'Oh, boy,' said Ziggy. 'Come on, Wally, run!'

Wally didn't move. 'Does this mean you don't have any grapefruit? How about the nuclear reactor thingie?'

'Get outta here!' yelled the clerk, continuing to charge with his broom. He collided with massive Wally and flew backwards into the shelves of paint. As the cans cascaded down, they popped open and showered him with twenty different colours of paint.

'You know,' Ziggy whispered to Wally, 'I don't think he's a very good clerk. Look at the mess he made.' He tore the list out of the clerk's hand and they raced out of the store.

'Hey, Ziggy,' panted Wally as they ran down the street. 'I've got an important question.'

'What is it?'

Wally said hopefully, 'Do I really look like Lydia the Lunatic?'

CHAPTER 13

THE JUNKYARD JOUST

On the outskirts of Pookesville, Si, Meese and Curly arrived at the junkyard owned by Irvin Dubowski. Mr Dubowski's smiling face was plastered on a large billboard over the entrance to the junkyard. In the picture on the billboard the owner was puffing on a large cigar and the caption read, I'VE NEVER MET JUNK I DIDN'T LIKE.

'Sounds like my kind of guy,' said Si happily. He and Meese were dressed in an orange jumpsuit with heavy work boots.

'Wowlookatthisplace,' said Curly, staring at the mountains of junk everywhere. Curly had on his football sweater, sweatpants and tennis shoes.

They watched as a pudgy man in a shiny suit came out of the stacks of junk and approached them. He held out his hand for Si.

'Irvin Dubowski,' he said, smiling and chomping on a cigar.

'I *know* that name,' cried out Si.

'It's the guy on the billboard!' said Meese in exasperation.

Dubowski pointed a finger at Si and smiled. 'I can tell you're gonna be a real tough negotiator, slick. I better watch myself.'

Si puffed out his chest. 'Well, I have been around the block a few times. Yessir, it'd be pretty tough to pull anything over on me.'

Dubowski held up his hands in mock surrender. 'I wouldn't dream of trying. Just make me look pretty silly going up against a smart feller like yourself.'

Meese whispered to Si. 'Watch out, I think he's trying to lull you into a false sense of security.'

Si laughed. 'Lull, shmull, he's just very perceptive of my outstanding deal-making abilities.'

Dubowski glanced over at Curly. 'You feeling OK, son, you look a little green.'

'I'mfinethankyoubutIdon'ttrustyou,' mumbled Curly.

'Uh huh,' said Dubowski, who obviously had no idea what Curly had just said. He looked back at Si. 'So what can I do for you?'

Curly handed him the list and Dubowski studied it. 'Steering wheel, check. Dashboard, we got that. Suede seats. Got a nice set right off of Elvis's own Cadillac. That'll cost you extra.'

'Elvis! Cool,' exclaimed Si.

Dubowski continued with the list. 'Muffler, check. AM/FM/CD player, OK. Yep, we got all this stuff.' He whistled at some workers in the yard and barked instructions. In a few minutes all the items had been assembled.

Dubowski took out a calculator and added everything up. 'OK, that'll be four thousand eight hundred and sixteen dollars.'

'What?!' said Meese. 'That can't be right.'

'Whoops, you know what? I did make a mistake,' said Dubowski. 'I forgot to add in the sales tax. It's actually an even five thousand dollars.'

'Great,' said Si. 'What a bargain.'

'Are you crazy?' said Meese. 'It's just a bunch of junk. Why, I bet all that stuff's not worth more than few dollars.'

Dubowski looked very offended. He rubbed his hand along the blue suede car seat. 'Why, this is the very seat where the King of Rock and Roll himself, the one and only Elvis Presley, situated his one and only posterior.'

'Yeah, Meese,' said Si. 'It's got the King's butt marks right on it. That's probably worth more than five thousand dollars all by itself.'

Dubowski slapped Si on the back. 'I knew I liked you, son. You've got style.'

Meese said, 'If Elvis Presley sat on that, then I'm a monkey's uncle.'

'Boy,' said Si, 'what fun you must have had swinging around those trees and eating all those bananas with your nephew.'

'I give up,' said Meese.

'We'll take it,' said Si. 'Here's our money.'

Dubowski took the cash, counted it slowly and then his round face flushed. 'We got ourselves a little problem here, fellers. This is only twelve dollars.'

Si slapped him on the back. 'Twelve dollars, five thousand dollars, what difference does it really make between friends?'

'The difference,' said Dubowski firmly, 'is four thousand nine hundred and eighty-eight dollars. And if you don't have it, you don't get any of this.'

'Well, what can we get for twelve dollars then?' asked Si.

Dubowski picked up the rusted muffler, tore off one corner and held it out. 'Here, you can have this for twelve bucks and consider it a gift.'

'Wow, thanks,' said Si, reaching for it, but Meese slapped his hand down.

'You can keep that thing. It's not worth twelve cents.'

'YeahsothereandImightstickoutmytongueatyoutoo,' mumbled Curly.

Dubowski glared at them. 'We got us a couple of special employees for dealing with customers like you.'

'Wow, special employees just for us,' said Si.

Dubowski whistled and they could all hear the sounds of something hurtling towards them.

Curly saw them first. 'Ohboythisdoesn'tlook-goodsodon'tevenlook.'

Two very large and very fierce guard dogs flashed around a corner of junk and headed right towards the Fries with their very big fangs bared.

'Get 'em, boys,' yelled Dubowski.

'YEOW!' yelled Si, and he took off, dragging Meese along. Curly started running too, but in a different direction. 'CatchmeifyoucanbutIdon'tthinkyoucan.'

The two dogs ran after Curly. The green Fry, however, was very, *very* fast, and the dogs were not gaining on him. In fact, he was so speedy he had to keep stopping to let the dogs catch up.

Curly flew up the side of a large crane and ran out onto its arm. Swinging around and around, he then let go, uncoiled his long arms and snagged a weathervane on top of the junkyard's office building. From there he sailed to the ground, did a forward roll, popped up, came around behind the two dogs and zoomed in circles around them so fast they finally fell over, dizzy, with their tongues hanging out.

Curly used a water hose to fill up a car hubcap he'd found on the ground. The dogs thirstily lapped up the water while the green Fry scratched them behind the ears. When they were done with the water, the dogs licked Curly's arm. He said, 'Comeonlet'sgoseemyfriends.'

When Dubowksi saw his dogs meekly following Curly, the cigar fell out of his mouth. From the top of the fence, Si yelled, 'Atta boy, Curly. You sure have a way with mean dogs.'

'They'renotmean,justmisunderstood,' mumbled Curly.

'Hey, you stupid dogs,' growled Dubowski. 'What do you think you're doing? I told you to sic 'em.' He cuffed one of them on the ear and it yelped.

'Don'thitthemagainorI'llhavetogetroughwith-you,' Curly warned him.

Dubowski walked over to Curly and balled up

his fists. 'They're my dogs and I'll treat 'em any way I want to.'

Curly looked at the dogs and mumbled, 'OK-guysgogethimbutnobodilyharm.'

The dogs started growling and moving towards Dubowski, who backed up, looking terrified.

'Ihopeyoucanrunreallyfast,' mumbled Curly.

With a scream, Dubowski took off running and the dogs flew after him.

Si and Meese jumped down from the fence and ran over to join Curly.

Si said, 'OK, let's get out of here while the getting is good.'

He made a move to leave, but Meese refused to budge.

'Meese, let's go before that guy gets back. I'm sure he just loves me because he could see what a great wheeler-dealer I am, but I don't think he likes you very much.'

'Give me the twelve dollars,' said Meese.

'What?'

'The twelve dollars, give it to me.'

Si handed him the money, and Meese laid it on the ground and put it a stone on it so it wouldn't blow away.

'What are you doing?' asked Si.

'Paying for this.' Meese picked up the blue suede car seat.

Si beamed. 'Meese, you *do* think it's true, don't you?'

'I don't know, but if Elvis Presley did sit his butt on this thing, I guess it's worth twelve bucks.'

The three streaked away while Irvin Dubowski ran screaming around the junkyard, the dogs right behind him.

CHAPTER 14

HAROLD RETURNS THE FAVOUR

Theodore, Freddy and Howie were hard at work on the time travel machine in Freddy's lab when the other Fries returned.

'Did you get everything on the lists?' asked Freddy.

While Ziggy shook his head sadly, Si held up the blue suede car seat. 'We got this super-duper seat,' said Si. 'Elvis sat on it. His butt marks are on there for all time.'

Freddy looked stunned. 'This is it?! We can't make the time machine work with only a blue suede car seat. We'll be laughed out of town.'

'Well, laughter *is* the best medicine,' observed Si with a big smile.

Freddy shook his head and sat down on the floor with his hands over his face.

'What are you doing?' asked Ziggy.

'I'm trying to think of a small island where I can go and hide for the rest of my life,' Freddy replied.

Just then the phone in Freddy's lab rang. He picked it up. 'Yes?'

'Freddy, it's Harold Pumpernickel. Your dad said I might find you around here. Can we talk about something?'

Freddy looked curiously at the others. 'Are you alone, Harold?'

'Absolutely. Adam doesn't even know I'm here.'

'OK, hold on.'

Freddy pulled a lever. There was a scream and Harold dropped down through the trapdoor and landed in a soft pile of hay. He stood and brushed himself off.

'Wow, cool lab, Freddy,' said Harold as he looked around at all of Freddy's equipment and inventions. He pointed to a pair of tennis shoes that hung on a peg.

'What do those do?'

'Show him, Howie,' said Freddy.

Howie put on the shoes and clicked the heels together.

VVRROOMM! He took off like a shot. The shoes made him run so fast that he was completely a blur. And he could run up walls and even across the ceiling. He stopped by clicking them together again.

'I call them the Red Rocket tennis shoes,' said Freddy.

'Powered by solar amplification with reverse modulating gravitational dynamics?' asked Harold.

'That's right,' replied Freddy. 'With just a

smidgen of diesel fuel thrown in. For catalytic purposes only,' he quickly added. Harold pointed to what looked like a Frisbee lying on Freddy's worktable. That doesn't look like an ordinary Frisbee.'

'It's not,' boomed Wally. He picked it up and flung it. The Frisbee soared around the room, and everyone put their hands over their noses.

'PHEW!' said Harold, 'that smells awful.'

Freddy caught the Frisbee. 'It should, it's the Stink Frisbee. So long as it's moving through the air it puts out a smell like month-old sweaty socks mixed with rotten eggs. When I'm really mad at my sister, I toss it in her window.'

'Cool,' Harold said again. Then he looked around the lab with a rueful expression. 'Boy, it'd be nice to have a place like this to invent things.'

'Well, you can come over any time you want,' offered Freddy. 'So what was it you wanted to tell me, Harold?'

'I wanted to thank you again for helping me on the volcano.'

'That's OK, Harold, we were glad to do it,' said Freddy. 'By the way, what propulsion device are you using for the volcano's eruption?'

'The ACME Turbo Booster 3000 with maximum velocity thruster and optional afterburner. It cost a lot of money, but Adam wanted the best.'

'I'm sure he did.'

'And I also wanted to thank you for having your dad hire my mom to work as a part-time cook at the Burger Castle.'

Freddy's eyes bugged out. 'I didn't know he'd hired your mother.'

'I thought it was your idea.'

'I wish it had been. She's a great cook.'

'Thanks,' said Harold, smiling. He looked at what they were working on. 'Is this *your* science project?'

'Yes, but we've run into a snag. We can't find the materials we need to build it,' said Freddy.

'What sort of stuff do you need?'

Freddy showed him the list. 'We tried at the hardware store and Dubowski's Junkyard, but they didn't have what we needed.'

'Well, I don't think we have a nuclear reactor turbine, but we have the other stuff,' said Harold.

'What do you mean?'

'My dad has a junkyard too, over near our

house. You wouldn't believe what people throw in the trash. My dad sorts through the stuff every week and keeps the things that he can sell or use. You can come over and take what you need.'

'We'll pay for it,' said Freddy.

'Yeah,' exclaimed Si. 'We've got twelve dollars.'

Meese poked him. 'No, we don't. We paid that for the Elvis seat.'

'Oh, yeah,' said Si. 'OK, we've got zip as far as cash goes.'

'You don't have to pay us, Freddy. You already helped me on my project. So now it's my turn to help you. So come on over and get the stuff you need.'

Freddy looked at the Fries and Howie. 'Let's go, gang. We don't have much time left.'

CHAPTER 15

ASK A LIBRARIAN

Freddy and the gang got just about everything they needed from Mr Pumpernickel's junkyard, including thousands of rivets, metal sheeting for the exterior of the time travel machine, super strong windows that had come off a demolished bank building and engine parts from a junked race car. Over the next three days they banged, molded, screwed, hammered and bent the time machine into shape.

'That magnetic transformer needs to be polarized in the opposite circuitry where it is presently in order to provide adequate navigational capability,' Theodore said to Wally.

The purple Fry stared at him blankly. 'HUH?'

Theodore sighed and said, 'Switch the blue and red wires so we can steer.'

'Gotcha, Teddio.'

Si, Meese and Curly put the blue suede Elvis seat in and bolted it down, and then Howie put in the steering wheel.

'How exactly do you steer through time?' Howie asked.

'Very carefully,' replied Theodore.

Freddy and Theodore examined the blueprints they had drawn up and then compared them with the plans in the logbook.

'It looks perfect,' said Theodore.

'Yeah, but we have two probleMs First, we don't have this thing.' He pointed to the drawings where a small object resembling a gyroscope sat on top of the time machine. 'According to the plans, that's the thing that creates the hole in the time-space continuum that will allow us to leave our time and go to another. But Finklebean doesn't say how to build it. Without that, it won't work.'

'OK, we've got the first problem nailed down; what's the second one, Freddio?' asked Si, cheerfully.

'The second problem is we still don't have a way to power the time machine,' Freddy added gloomily. 'And without those two things it's just a big lump of metal. And the science competition is tomorrow. I don't know what we're going to do. I'm out of answers.'

Howie snapped his fingers. 'Questions and answers? Remember, Freddy? It's "Ask A Librarian Week". Maybe that lady at the library can help us. And she *knew* Silas Finklebean.'

'Well,' said Theodore. 'Perhaps she can help.'

Freddy sighed. 'We don't have anything to lose, I guess.'

Freddy and Howie rode their bikes down to the library. Inside they found the librarian working at the front desk.

'Can I help you, boys?' she said pleasantly.

'Uh, yes, Ms, uh . . . ,' began Freddy.

'Oh, where are my manners. My name is Mildred Maraschino.'

'OK, Ms Maraschino. We were wondering if you could tell us anything else about Silas Finklebean.'

'Like what?'

'Well, you said he was a very lucky person. And that he was very generous.'

'That's right, he was. And he loved children. They were his best friends actually. All the adults thought he was, well, not exactly right in the head.'

'That happens to me and my dad all the time,' replied Freddy, knowingly. 'Did you know much about his inventions?'

Mildred hesitated, eyeing the boys closely. 'I was very young back then. I do remember that he was a very careful man. He planned for every possibility.'

'That's what my dad taught me too,' said

Freddy. 'Every scientist has to think that way. You have to be responsible, but you still can have fun.'

'I think you and Silas would've gotten on very well,' said Mildred, smiling. She hesitated and then plucked something out of her desk drawer. 'Silas gave me this.' She held it up. It was a small mirror. 'He said this was a wishing mirror. He told me if you looked into it and concentrated very hard, you could make a wish and it would come true.'

'Boy, I could use one of those,' said Freddy.

'I've tried to make it work over the years, but I guess I wasn't doing it right. My wish never came true,' she added sadly. She handed the mirror to Freddy.

He looked into it and then concentrated very hard. What he was wishing for was an answer to their dilemma. *I need to find that gyroscope device. I need to find that gyroscope device.* He said this to himself over and over. Nothing happened, though, and he finally handed the mirror back.

'Silas must've really liked you to give you a wishing mirror, even if it didn't work right,' said Howie.

'I think of all the children he knew, he liked me the best,' she replied. 'I don't think he gave anyone else anything he'd made.'

Freddy thought for a moment and then it struck him. 'Did Silas ever give you something else? Maybe something to keep safe for him?'

Mildred looked taken aback. 'Why do you ask that?'

'Because you said he planned for every possibility. And you said you were the only one he ever gave anything he'd made. I bet he trusted you.'

Mildred looked a little uncomfortable, but finally, she said, 'I live just down the street. Would you boys like to see something?'

They both nodded.

A few minutes later they were walking into Mildred's little cottage. It was cozy inside with lots of dainty knick-knacks everywhere. Mildred excused herself. While she was gone Freddy looked over some old family pictures on the fireplace mantel. One of them surprised him. He was about to say something to Howie but then Mildred came back into the room holding a small box.

'Is that what Silas wanted you to keep safe?' Freddy said, pointing at the box.

Mildred nodded, put the box on the coffee table and opened it. Freddy and Howie looked at each other excitedly. It was the gyroscope-like thing from the time machine plans.

'What did he say when he gave that to you?' asked Freddy.

Mildred closed her eyes and her brow wrinkled

as she thought hard. 'He told me that it held the key to everyone's future. And that he wouldn't trust it with an adult, but that it would be safe with a child. I never knew what he meant by that.' She opened her eyes and continued, 'Do you?'

Freddy could hardly contain his excitement. 'I think I know exactly what he meant. Ms Maraschino, do you mind if we borrow it?'

She put her hand protectively on top of the device. 'I'm not sure.'

'We'll take good care of it, I promise,' said Freddy.

'I've never let this out of my possession since he gave it to me.'

Freddy glanced over at the pictures on the mantel and then turned back to her. 'If you let us take it, I think that the next wish you make in your wishing mirror might just come true. And Silas did say it would be safe with a child.'

Mildred still looked unsure. 'My wish? How can you –'

'Just trust me, Ms Maraschino,' said Freddy. 'I know I'm just a kid, but I'm also a scientist, a very trustworthy one.'

Mildred looked doubtful for a moment, and then she finally said, 'Well, until you both came along no one seemed to care about Silas anymore, which was very sad indeed. So, yes, you can take it.'

As Freddy took the box, Mildred added, 'Do you think you'll be able to find your future with it?'

Freddy patted the box. 'I think our future looks really bright now.'

CHAPTER 16

THE POWER OF PURPLE AND BLUE

Freddy and Howie got back to the lab, and with the help of the Fries they were able to attach the device Mildred had given them to the time machine.

'There,' said Freddy with a final turn of the wrench.

Theodore was looking at the plans. 'Well, we have everything in place. The only problem is we have no way to power up the time machine.'

'I know,' said Freddy miserably.

While no one was looking, Wally had slipped behind some junk they hadn't used and took a bottle from a hiding place. It was the liquid blue stuff he'd found in Finklebean's lab.

'OK, Freddy said I shouldn't do this, so I'm not,' he said to himself. 'No matter how much I want to or how good it tastes or how thirsty little, skinny Wally is, I'm not going to drink it, because that would be bad – very, very bad.'

He took the top off the bottle and sniffed.

'Right – no matter how good it smells, no matter how much fun it is to drink this blue stuff, Wally is not gonna do it, because I promised my special friend and buddy, Freddy, that I wouldn't – and friends always keep their promises.'

Wally tipped the bottle up to his mouth.

'And another thing,' he continued, whispering to himself, 'A friend who can't keep a promise to another friend is just no stinking good. I mean, how can a friend do that to another friend? A promise is a promise and Wally never, ever breaks a promise.'

Wally tipped the bottle all the way up and took a long chug, wiped his mouth and put the top back on. 'Whew, that was close. But like I said, a promise is a prom– YEOW!' Wally flew up into the air and crashed into the ceiling of the lab. Then he shot down, hit the floor and zoomed forward.

Freddy and the rest of the gang threw themselves in all directions as the big purple Fry whizzed around the room like a ball in a pinball machine, knocking over shelves, smashing equipment and punching holes in walls. For twenty minutes they all watched as the purple blob whizzed around the room faster and faster.

Finally, Wally came crashing down. The lab lay in ruin. Everyone stood and gathered angrily around him.

He started muttering, 'Wally is a good Fry. Wally kept his promise. No blue stuff.' He opened his eyes and looked up at them. 'Hey, guys, is it lunchtime yet?'

Ziggy scolded, 'Wally, you drank the blue stuff and destroyed Freddy's lab.'

'What do you have to say for yourself?' added Theodore severely.

Wally sat up, looking confused. 'Now wait just a minute. Are you sure it was *me*? There are other Fries in the room too, you know.'

'Enormous and purple narrows it down considerably,' said Theodore.

'And,' squeaked Ziggy, 'there's the blue bottle right there in your hand.'

Wally held up the bottle. 'I've never seen this before.' His eyes got really big. 'It must have been *planted* on me. Oh, my gosh, there's a conspiracy going on. People are out to get me.'

'Why would anyone want to get *you*, Wally?' said Howie.

Wally threw up his big hands. 'Don't you see, Howie? They're jealous. I mean, look at me: Tall, handsome, smart and PURPLE. But I want whoever did it to know this!' He paused, put a hand over his heart and said in a high-pitched, choked voice, 'I forgive you.' He wiped a tear away.

Theodore looked over at Freddy. 'Well, Freddy, you haven't said anything. What do you think his punishment should be? Freddy?'

Freddy was staring off into space. He obviously hadn't been listening to any of their conversation.

'Uh, Freddy,' said Theodore gently.

'EUREKA!' shouted Freddy and he jumped straight up in the air. Then he gave Wally a big hug. 'You big, beautiful purple Fry you. You're brilliant!'

He grabbed the blue bottle from Wally and raced to his work area.

Wally looked at the other Fries. 'Well, I'm glad to see at least someone here recognizes genius.' He walked away with his head held high, tripped and landed upside down inside an old tractor tyre.

The other Fries hustled over to where Freddy was working frantically.

'Freddy,' said Theodore, 'Why are you so excited?'

Freddy held up the blue bottle. 'This, Theodore, this.'

'The blue stuff?' said Si. 'OK, it's blue and it's wet, but even for a happy Fry like me, it's not all that exciting, Freddio.'

'Oh, it's very exciting,' said Freddy. 'It's the most exciting thing to happen to me since I invented all of you.'

'What do you mean?' asked Theodore. 'How can that blue liquid be so important?'

'Because *this* is what's going to power our time travel machine.'

CHAPTER 17

THE PRIMO FAKEOUT

'Freddy,' called out Nancy, who was standing on the trapdoor to Freddy's lab. 'Oh, Freddy, dear, I'd like to take a tour of the Nancy S. Funkhouser Imperial Theatre and Museum, and I'd like it right *now*.'

'Great,' said Freddy with a scowl. He was putting the finishing touches on the time travel machine.

When he didn't answer, she said, 'I know you're in there, Freddy. I'll give you two hours. If the theatre isn't done, then I'm telling dad about that secret passageway under the Burger Castle and that you're up to something.' They heard her stomp away.

Freddy shook his head wearily. 'Look,' he said, staring at Si, Meese, Wally, Curly and Ziggy. 'You guys are going to have to do something with her.'

'Like what?' asked Si. 'Tell her a joke? I'm terrific at jokes.'

'The only one who laughs at your jokes is you,' said Meese.

'See, that's what I mean,' said Si. 'That proves how funny I am. I'm a tough critic.'

'What I want you to do,' said Freddy, 'is somehow convince her that the stupid museum and theatre is almost done.'

'It is?' said Wally. 'I didn't even know we'd been working on it.'

'We haven't,' squeaked Ziggy. 'We have to make her believe that we have.'

'I knew that,' said Wally quickly. 'OK, let's go trick her.'

'Wally,' said Freddy, 'do you have a plan as to how you're going to do that?'

'Uh,' said Wally. 'That would be a no.'

'Wait a minute, I've got a plan,' said Si. 'A great plan. I read it in a book and it worked like a charm.'

'You're sure?' said Freddy.

'Piece of cake. Just leave it to me.'

Two hours later, after a lot of hard work down in the secret area under the Burger Castle, Si, Meese, Ziggy and Wally admired what they'd accomplished.

They had hung huge canvases on the walls and painted colourful scenes on them. In bright lights was a big marquee that read, THE NANCY S. FUNKHOUSER IMPERIAL THEATRE. And there was a large picture of Nancy next to it dressed up in a fancy costume. A door into the theatre had massive windows, and through them one could see the ticket counters and refreshment stand and the double doors leading into the theatre.

On another canvas they had painted a sign that read: THE NANCY S. FUNKHOUSER MUSEUM. Here were portraits of Nancy and windows through which one could see costumes displayed in glass boxes. Also visible through a window was a shop where you could buy coffee mugs and T-shirts. It all looked three-dimensional, like you could walk right in.

'Do you think she'll believe it's real?' squeaked Ziggy.

'Sure,' said Si. 'It worked great in the book. And it'll work great here.'

'What was the book?' asked Meese.

'*The Emperor's New Clothes*,' replied Si.

'Uhohthere'ssomebodycomingandIthinkit'syou-knowwho,' mumbled Curly.

'Quick, to your places,' cried Si. 'And, action!'

When Nancy arrived, she saw Wally in his Wilma costume sweeping the entrance to the theatre. Ziggy was busy washing windows, while Curly was on a ladder pretending to adjust the lights on the marquee. Si and Meese were polishing the knobs on the front doors.

Nancy's eyes grew so huge it didn't seem like her face had room for them.

'Oh, my gosh,' she said breathlessly. 'It's . . . it's beautiful. *I'm* beautiful,' she added, looking up at her picture. 'I can't wait to go inside.'

She took a step towards the doors, but Si stopped her. 'Uh, that's not a good idea.'

'Why not?'

'It's bad luck to go inside for the first time except on opening night.'

'It is?' asked Nancy.

'Absolutely,' said Si. 'I'm sure an actress with your experience knows that.'

'Right, of course I do,' said Nancy hastily.

'And that way on opening night all of your adoring fans will be in their seats to see you for the first time in your very own theatre.'

Nancy looked starry-eyed. 'Well, I better go and start rehearsing. I'm thinking of playing all the parts in *Romeo and Juliet*.'

After she'd rushed off, Ziggy looked at Si. 'You pulled it off.'

'You mean you had doubts?' the happy red Fry said. 'Like I said, piece of cake.'

'Oh yeah?' said a gloomy Meese.

'Come on, Meese, why the pout? She bought the story hook, line and sinker.'

'That's right, she did. For now! But what about when she comes back for opening night, tries to go through the doors, and runs right into the wall. What then, Mr Genius?'

'By then I'll have left the country,' said Si, grinning.

'Well,' said Meese, 'at least you're not as stupid as you look.'

CHAPTER 18

TESTING TIME

The time travel machine was ready to test.

'OK,' said Freddy. He carefully poured some of the blue liquid into a special tank he'd built as part of the time machine. 'Now I've set it up so the blue fuel won't ignite until it's combined with liquid nitrogen. That'll happen when I push the GO button inside the time travel machine.'

'Wow, Freddy,' said Howie. 'This is so cool. We're really going to travel through time.'

'That's the general idea,' said Freddy. He picked up three football helmets and handed one to Howie and another to Theodore.

'What's this for?' asked Howie.

'In case something goes wrong.'

'Will something go wrong?' he asked nervously.

'I don't know, Howie. That's why we wear the helmets.'

They climbed in and sat on the Elvis blue suede seat, and Freddy closed the hatch-like door. They went through their checklists like pilots did before a flight.

'Check-check-check-check and double check,' said Howie in answer to Freddy's questions. 'We are roger wilco and ready to GO-GO.'

'OK, Theodore,' said Freddy, 'engage the time dial.'

Theodore set the time dial for five minutes earlier. He nodded at Freddy, who took a deep breath and hit the GO button.

Instantly, there was a feeling of tremendous speed and blazing colours right outside the machine. As they looked out they could make out a swirl of things moving, like people and buildings. Freddy and Howie screamed once when something flashed next to the window. It looked like a large bird, but it was flying upside down.

'Look!' cried Howie. 'That looks like the earth.'

Sure enough, right outside was a large shape

that looked just like the earth. And just beyond it was a far larger shape.

'That's the sun,' exclaimed Freddy. 'Wait a minute. The earth is going around the sun, but it's going around it backwards. Because we're moving *back* in time!'

Then there was a humming sound, and they could feel themselves slowing down. A few seconds later the machine came to a smooth stop and everything was calm again. They peered outside.

'Oh, my gosh,' said Freddy. He was staring at himself, Howie and Theodore. Freddy was just pouring the blue stuff into the time machine and he was speaking the exact words he had spoken five minutes earlier.

They all looked at each other in stunned silence. Finally, they all cried out together. 'It works! It works! We did it!' They high-fived each other, and Theodore even gave Howie a couple of head noogies.

After they had calmed down, Freddy set the time dial for the time they had left and hit GO. They were instantly blasted by waves of colour again. Things swooped and darted by the windows.

As they were watching this the strange humming sound started again and they cruised to a smooth stop.

Freddy shouted, 'We can go anywhere in time that we want! We can see everything.'

Suddenly, Howie's eyes got really huge. 'Freddy, do you know what that means? If we go into the future, we'll know things before they even happened. Like, I could see the answers on the math test and then come back and get a hundred.'

'Howie, that would be cheating,' scolded Freddy.

'That's just because you always get hundreds anyway. But you could go into the future and see what'll happen to you. And if you don't like it, you could change it.'

Theodore said sternly, 'Changing the future can have very serious repercussions.'

'That's right, Howie,' said Freddy. 'Besides, we have something else to worry about right now. Remember the volcano? Adam's going to use it to cover the Burger Castle in goop.'

'That's right!' exclaimed Howie. 'I know. If he does, we can go back in the time machine and change it.'

Freddy chuckled. 'I don't need the time machine to take care of Adam and his stupid volcano. I'd say *his* future looks pretty bad.'

CHAPTER 19

THE SPANKER SWITCHEROO

Late that night Freddy, Howie and the Fries snuck back to the Burger Castle after it had closed. Howie and Freddy put on dark outfits and covered their faces with masks. Then the two boys put on their Red Rocket tennis shoes.

'We look like burglars,' said Howie.

Wally said nervously, 'Burglars?'

Theodore answered, 'Yes. Felonious types who pursue their malfeasance on an unsuspecting public.'

Wally looked relieved. 'Whew, and here I was thinking they were bad guys who stole from people.'

'OK, guys, here's the plan,' said Freddy as he handed walkie-talkies to all of them. They huddled together.

A few minutes later Freddy and Howie slipped out from the bushes around the Burger Castle and headed across the street to the Patty Cakes. They reached the parking lot of Patty Cakes and then hit the ground well away from the completed volcano that now towered over the restaurant, huge and scary.

Freddy pulled out a pair of binoculars and looked around. He saw two of Adam's gang guarding the volcano. Freddy looked at Howie next to him. 'OK, time for the diversionary tactic.' He spoke into his walkie-talkie. 'Ready, guys?' said Freddy.

'READY!' said a voice back.

'Go!' said Freddy.

A minute later down the street came Theodore dressed in a top hat and a red jumper suit, with big black boots. He carried a baton that he was twirling. Under his top hat was a small CD player. When Theodore touched the top button of his red jumper suit, loud marching band music started playing.

Behind Theodore was Wally dressed up as a very large clown, holding a rope. At the end of that rope floated Si and Meese. They had held their breaths, which caused a chemical reaction in their bodies, producing helium.

Behind them came Curly, who was wearing a very long shirt and had risen twenty feet up into the air, as though he were on stilts. He was tossing something into the air and then catching it. It was Ziggy, made up and painted to look like a volleyball. Ziggy screamed with laughter every time he went sailing up in the air.

Adam's two guards looked over at all the commotion.

'Wow,' said one of them, 'It's a parade. Come on!'

'Wait a minute,' said the other boy. 'Whoever heard of a parade at night?'

Right then Theodore called out loudly, 'All right, everyone, let's have a good practice for the real parade tomorrow. But we really need some volunteers to test our super special tricks with.'

The two boys looked at each other. 'Super special tricks!' they exclaimed together. When they raced away to join the practice parade, Freddy and Howie jumped up.

'OK, engage Red Rocket tennis shoes,' instructed Freddy.

Both Freddy and Howie clicked the red tennis shoes they were wearing.

VRROOMM! They shot across the street and up the sides of the volcano, disappearing into the opening. They clicked their shoes again and stopped.

'Wow,' said Howie, catching his breath, 'Can I use these shoes when I run track?'

'That would be cheating, Howie.'

'I know that, so what's your point?'

Freddy examined the machinery that would make the volcano erupt. 'OK, it's just like Harold said, an ACME Turbo Booster 3000 with the special option package.' He studied the directional control and the instructions contained in a small sign over it. 'According to the instructions, I just have to turn the control knob forty-five degrees counterclockwise to aim it where I want it.' Freddy turned the knob. 'There, that should do it.'

'You have it pointed at the Patty Cakes restaurant so it'll get creamed, right?' said Howie.

'No, I set it so it'll just shoot straight up and then down the sides of the volcano like it was supposed to.'

'But Adam was going to cover the Burger Castle in goop, so why not get him back?'

'You remember what Adam said; he'll blame Harold.'

'Good point.'

'OK, it's all set. Make sure the coast is clear.'

Howie peered over the lip of the volcano.

'Oh, my gosh!' he exclaimed.

'What?' said Freddy.

'Look!'

Curly was tossing one of Adam's gang into the air. The other kid was being held upside down by the floating Si and Meese. Apparently both boys were having a ball, because even from here Howie and Freddy could hear them laughing.

'The Fries sure know how to have a good time,' said Freddy, smiling. 'OK, engage Red Rocket tennis shoes.'

They clicked their heels together.

VVRROOMM! They shot out of the volcano, down the sides and across the street in a matter of seconds.

When they were safely back at the Burger Castle, Howie said, 'Aw, come on, Freddy. Let me wear these on the track team, please!'

'No, Howie.' Freddy pulled out his walkie-talkie and spoke into it. 'OK, mission accomplished. Cease diversionary tactic.'

The Fries played with the boys for a little bit longer and then marched back down the street. They joined Howie and Freddy right after that while the gang members went back to guard the volcano.

'Thanks, guys,' said Freddy. 'It worked to perfection.'

But after they left, Adam Spanker came out of hiding near the volcano and told his gang members to go home. He climbed into the mouth of the volcano and looked at the instructions to aim the eruption. 'Funky, when this baby blows, you and the Burger Dump are history.'

CHAPTER 20

A MATTER OF TIME

The morning of the science competition was nice and sunny. Because the Patty Cakes parking lot was so large, it was being used to hold the competition. Plus, the volcano was so big it couldn't be moved anyway. Freddy's father had put the time travel machine on the back of a trailer and hauled it to the parking lot. Dozens of other kids and their parents were showing up with their science projects. It became clear quickly, though, that the volcano was the one to beat.

'Hi, Harold,' said Freddy as he passed by the volcano where Harold was putting on some finishing touches.

'Hey, Freddy. My mom baked a bunch of goodies for everybody. You should go get some.'

'I can smell them from here. Good luck in the competition.'

'Good luck to you too, Freddy.'

Freddy walked over to Mrs Pumpernickel and got some cookies. At that instant the Fries showed up along with Howie. The Fries weren't wearing their disguises because they'd been entertaining the crowd like they did at the Burger Castle.

'They just love seeing me and Meese floating like ballons,' said Si. 'We're the best.'

'Speak for yourself,' moaned Meese. 'I'm not the best, I'm the worst.'

Wally sniffed the aroma of Mrs Pumpernickel's cooking and rubbed his belly.

'OOOOHHHH BBBOOYY! Me love everything in the whole world.'

He grabbed a bunch of cookies, two cakes and four pies, and would have eaten everything else including the table the food was on if Freddy hadn't stopped him.

'OK, guys,' said Freddy. 'It's time to get to work.'

They headed over to the time machine. Standing near it was an elderly woman. As they drew closer Freddy recognized her. It was Mildred Maraschino.

'Quite an interesting machine you have here,' she said.

'Thanks, Ms Maraschino,' said Freddy.

'I see you found a use for the thing you borrowed,' she said, pointing at the gyroscope on top of the time machine.' She paused and asked, 'So what exactly does it do?'

'Well, actually, it's kind of based on some plans of Silas Finklebean's that we found,' explained Freddy.

'I was hoping you would say that,' said Ms Maraschino.

'What?' asked Freddy.

'I wish you the very, very best of luck, Freddy,' she said, smiling. 'Goodbye.' As she quickly walked off, Freddy stared after her until his gaze caught on something else. Across from the time machine, Stewie and Adam Spanker were standing proudly in front of the volcano while a photographer from the *Pookesville Tattler* took their picture. All around the volcano Adam's gang was positioned, armed with paintball guns.

Freddy looked angry. 'They don't even have Harold in the picture and he did all the work.'

'And look at Adam's goons all over the place,' added Howie.

However, Freddy wasn't listening. 'Nanny Boo-Boo?' He said as he stared at the person walking up to him. She was wearing a long trench coat with the collar turned up and big sunglasses. She slid the glasses down her nose, and Freddy saw that it was indeed his sister.

'Why are you dressed like that?' he asked.

In her British accent she said, 'You silly boy, so

my fans won't recognize me. Do you realize how hard it is for someone like me to go out in public?'

'Yeah, well, it's not so easy on the public either,' said Freddy.

'Hmmpphh! I guess I have to be somewhat nice to you since you did build me a wonderful theatre and museum. But remember, you unimportant little peon, my good nature does have its limit,' she added, and flounced off.

Alfred Funkhouser joined them. 'It's going to be hard to beat that volcano, son.'

'Don't worry, Dad, after I take the judges on a little trip we'll have this contest in the bag.'

'Look!' yelled Si. 'They're about to make the volcano erupt.'

Freddy looked at Howie and winked.

'Boy, the Spankers are in for a real surprise,' said Freddy.

Harold stood off to one side holding a remote control while Adam held up his hand and faced the crowd. 'And now I will have my very junior and very inexperienced assistant push the button on that . . . um . . . thingie to make the volcano . . . um . . . blow up.'

'Do you mean this electronic digitized wireless remote transponder unit that's required to engage the eruption phase of the volcano?' asked Harold with a little grin as he held up the device.

'Yeah!' snapped Adam with a menacing glare at Harold. Then he turned back, gave the crowd a wide, fake smile, and said in a pleasant voice, 'Yes, exactly, *junior assistant*. I should know, since I invented it, as well as this.' He swept his arm in the direction of the towering volcano as the crowd applauded.

'OK, here we go,' said Harold, and he pushed a button on the remote control.

At first there was nothing except some tiny gurgles. The next sound was a groan and not a very loud one. The crowd started getting antsy and Adam looked angrily at Harold. But then came a huge *GROAN*, like an elephant with a bellyache, and Adam started grinning. Next, the ground started to vibrate, and people in the crowd began eyeing each other nervously.

An instant later came a spine-tingling shriek from the volcano, like a thousand infants wanting a bottle of milk. Terrified kids in the crowd jumped into their parents' arMs After that, the volcano shook and quivered like it was trying to hold something back but couldn't.

Everyone in the crowd screamed when a huge wave of purple goop burst out of the volcano's top and shot thirty feet into the air, coating a flock of birds passing by.

Ziggy turned to Wally and said, 'Hey, that looks like you when you've had too much to eat.'

Wally watched with wide eyes at this purple tidal wave. 'OOOHHH, I think I'm in love.'

They all stared as the purple goop exploded up, up, up, and then suddenly turned and shot directly at the Patty Cakes restaurant.

'NOOO!' screamed Stewie Spanker. He was standing in front of the restaurant and the purple goop hit him so hard he was swept away. The purple wave kept on going, covering every square inch of the Patty Cakes, and then the volcano fell silent.

Howie and Freddy looked at each other worriedly. 'Oh, boy,' said Freddy, 'Did I mess up when I aimed the goop?'

Adam was still standing there, his stupid fake smile frozen on his lips. Finally, he looked over at the now-purple Patty Cakes, saw his purple father struggling to stand up and then pointed a fat finger at Freddy and roared, 'This is your doing, Funky Funkerhouser! You messed up my science project and now I'm going to destroy you!' He turned and spotted his gang in the stunned crowd. 'Get 'em,' yelled Adam.

Spanker's gang surged forward with their paintball guns.

'Uh-oh,' said Freddy. 'Something tells me this is not going to be good.'

'Good? We're going to die,' said Howie. 'And even worse, I'm almost out of cheese cubes.'

Alfred Funkhouser stepped forward and held up his hands to the charging gang.

'Now, boys . . .'

They flew right past him.

Stewie Spanker staggered out of the purple swamp his restaurant had become and roared, 'I want all the Funkhousers arrested.'

'What for?' said a stunned Alfred.

'For turning my restaurant purple and sticky, that's what, you maniac!'

Suddenly Nancy Funkhouser shot in front of Adam's gang. She put up a hand and spoke in a very deep, dramatic voice.

'I beseech you to cease and desist your barbaric behavior. When good confronts evil there can only be one outcome. Good shall triumph like a thunderbolt from the sky. So again, I implore you to rethink your evil ways and turn your actions instead towards the good of all.'

'Turn *this*!' yelled one of Spanker's gang and he nailed Nancy in the face with a green paintball. The gang raced on towards Freddy, Howie and the Fries.

'AAAHHH!' yelled Howie and Freddy as they turned and ran, along with the terrified Fries.

'OhboyIdon'tthinkwe'regoingtogetaway,' mumbled Curly.

'Yeah, it looks like we're dead meat for sure,' said Si cheerfully.

'Doomed, doomed, doomed,' moaned Meese. 'And I'm so young.'

'Yeah, and I'm so good-looking,' said Si. 'But you don't hear me complaining.'

'This way, guys,' yelled Freddy as the Spanker gang closed in.

Freddy had a way out of this, the only way out, in fact. He reached the time machine and popped open the hatch. 'Get in!' he yelled.

'But we can't all fit,' said Howie.

'Oh, yes we can,' boomed Wally. He scooped all of them up as he ran forward and an instant later they all were all crammed inside the machine.

'Quick, close the hatch,' yelled Freddy, who was smooshed against the other side and couldn't reach the control.

Theodore managed to stretch out his arm and hit the button. The hatch closed an instant before the Spanker gang reached it.

'Ready, aim, fire!' roared Adam.

The gang fired their paintballs at the time machine, but they did no damage.

'Ha-ha,' laughed Howie. 'You guys can't touch us.'

Wally, who was closest to the control panel, started poking at the buttons and switches.

'Wally,' said Theodore, 'whatever you do, do *not* hit the button marked GO.'

'What, this one?' said Wally as he pressed that very button.

'AAAAHHHHH!' they all yelled as the machine raced off to somewhere in time.

CHAPTER 21

THE FUTURE NOW

Everyone inside the time machine watched as swirls of rainbow colours shot outside the window.

'Look,' said Howie, pointing. 'That looks like a plane, only a really strange one. It doesn't have any wings.'

'It looks more like a car flying,' said Freddy.

'And there's a gigantic ice-cream cone,' said Wally, his face pressed against the window and drool running down his chin.

'Wally,' said Theodore, 'that looks more like a tornado than an ice-cream cone.'

'I love tornadoes,' replied Wally. 'They're yummy with sprinkles.'

'Over there,' said Howie. 'It's the earth and the sun thing again.'

'Only now it's moving in the other direction, really fast,' said Freddy.

'Which means that we're going into the *future*,' stated Theodore.

'Look,' said Freddy, 'there's a little boy. And he's FLYING. And over there it looks like a –'

This time the time travel machine came to a stop so fast everyone inside was pitched forward and slammed against the windshield.

'Where are we?' asked Howie as he peered out the window.

Freddy was looking out too. 'What does the time dial say?'

Theodore examined it. 'The year 2206.'

'Omigosh!' said Freddy. 'We went two hundred years into the future. How did the dial get set to that year?'

Wally started wailing. 'Oh, no, no, it can't be, not two hundred years into the future.'

'What are you so worked up about?' asked Si.

'Yeah, I'm the complainer around here,' moaned Meese. 'You're cramping my style.'

Wally looked at them tearfully. 'Don't you *get* it? I've *missed* two hundred years' worth of meals.'

'I'm sure they have a cornucopia of gastronomic delights in this century, Wally,' said Theodore.

'Yeah, but do they have FOOD?'

'That *is* food,' said Ziggy.

'Oh, OK, then,' said a relieved Wally. 'All that travel made me really hungry. Let's go get some corn-, corn-, corn and copies of gassy devil lights, like Theodore said.' He hit the lever for the hatch and it opened.

'Wait, Wally,' said Freddy, 'we don't know what's out there.'

'Only way to find out is to go exploring,' said Si as he and Meese hopped out.

'I think we should go back home,' said Theodore.

'Come on, Freddy,' said Howie. 'Remember? We can find out how we turned out.'

Freddy beamed. 'Wow, that would be cool. OK, come on.' They all climbed out of the machine. 'Wait a minute,' said Freddy. He pulled a small device out of his pocket and pointed it at the time machine. He hit a button and the time machine disappeared.

'Cool, Freddy,' said Howie.

'It's based on my Dad's Invisibrella invention. I figured if we went travelling through time we wouldn't want anyone messing with our machine while we're out of it.'

They moved away from the time machine and drew close to a bunch of buildings that were made of very shiny chrome and were tall and skinny. As they peered around a corner, they all got a shock.

Hundreds of people whizzed along – *three feet above the street*. Some were dressed in tight-fitting white outfits with black boots, others in burly coats with *sandals* on their feet. One group wore brightly coloured clothes with their hair fashioned in the shapes of ducks, ships and bowls of spaghetti. Another group were dressed as chess pieces and chased each other along the streets doing loop-the-loops.

'Wow, crazy clothes and crazy folks,' said Si. 'I love 'em.'

'They're scaring me out of my brain,' moaned Meese.

'Well, that shouldn't take long,' added Si.

'Those look like anti-gravity belts they're wearing,' said Freddy, 'only a lot more sophisticated than the ones we have.'

'Look at those vehicles,' said Theodore, pointing. Flying along next to the people were large rainbow-coloured contraptions with lots of people sitting inside.

'They must be like our buses,' said Howie.

'Come on,' said Freddy. 'It's time we checked out the future.'

'But what if someone sees us?' said Theodore.

Freddy replied, 'I never thought I'd say this, but from all the crazy things I've seen so far, we actually look pretty normal.'

They drew close to one of the rainbow buses, and it immediately stopped and lowered to the ground. The door opened and a robot driver addressed them. 'Where would you like to go?'

Freddy looked around at the others. 'Uh, I'm not sure.'

'The library!' cried Howie.

'Library?' said the robot. 'That term is not in my destination databank.'

'You know, where they have books and things,' said Freddy.

'Books?' said the robot.

Theodore, who was studying everything very closely, said, 'I think what my young friends mean is we would like to go to your place of knowledge and wisdom.'

'Ah, the Centre of Enlightenment, at the corner of Celsius and Andromeda. Please take a seat.'

As they boarded, Freddy said sheepishly, 'Uh, we don't have any money.'

'Money?' said the robot.

'Yeah, you know, to pay for the ride.'

The robot hit a button and the doors shut. 'The ride is free. Everything is free in Pookesville.'

They all stared at each other and then looked out the window as the bus shot off, causing them all to tumble into their seats.

'*This* is Pookesville?' said Howie.

'Look,' said Theodore as they flew past an intersection.

They stared out the window. Sure enough, sitting in the town square was the statue of Captain Peter Pookes, who had founded the town.

'Of course,' said Freddy. 'When we went into the future we did so only chronologically and stayed in the same place.'

Howie stared out the window at all the strange

buildings and people. 'Boy, things can change a lot in a couple hundred years.'

The bus dropped them off at the Centre of Enlightenment, a huge building that looked like a model of Earth. As Wally was getting off the bus, he stopped next to the robot.

'Hey, buddy, you wouldn't happen to have any food for a starving Fry, would you? I haven't had a thing to eat in over *two hundred years*.'

'Certainly,' replied the robot, and he handed Wally a pill the size of an aspirin.

Wally looked very disappointed. 'You don't have anything in super size, do you?'

The robot said, 'Don't eat it all at once. Goodbye.'

The bus took off, leaving Wally looking very depressed. He studied the pill, shrugged and then popped it in his mouth. 'At least it tastes good,' he said. Suddenly, his eyes grew huge and his belly shot straight out two feet. 'WWWOOOWWWW!!!' he shouted, rubbing his enormous stomach. I feel like I just ate all the food in the world.' He added tearfully, 'Me love the future.'

'Come on, Wally,' said Freddy, and they headed into the building.

Inside they quickly found that there were no books. All one had to do was sit in front of a small screen that was at each desk and say the name of a subject, and all the information about the subject would appear on the screen.

Howie sat down at one of the screens with a very determined look. 'OK, I want the winning numbers for all the Powerball lotteries for the years 2006 through 2050.' The numbers flashed on the screen and Howie started writing them down.

'Howie!' said Freddy sharply. 'What do you think you're doing?'

'Creating my own personal gold mine,' answered Howie happily. 'Do you have any idea how many cheese cubes I can buy with all the money I'm going to win?'

'But that's cheating.'

'It's only cheating if someone catches me.'

'Howie, you can't do that.'

Howie looked at Freddy's screen and said, 'All the plans for all the greatest inventions for the last hundred years.' The screen started filling up with information.

'WOW!' said a wide-eyed Freddy. 'This is so cool. Do you realize what I can do with this? I can go back to our time and build this stuff and help the whole world.'

Howie beamed. 'And you'll be the most famous inventor of all time. You'll knock Edison right off the top spot.'

'Wow,' said Freddy again. 'Freddy Funkhouser number one, Thomas Edison, a distant second.'

'Uh, Freddy?' said Theodore.

'Not now, Theodore, I need to print these plans out.'

'But, Freddy, haven't you thought about what you and Howie are doing?'

'Of course,' said Howie. 'We're taking full advantage of our situation for purposes of pure greed.'

'And world fame,' added Freddy.

'I think someone else might have travelled down this same path of temptation,' said Theodore.

'Who's that?' asked Freddy absently.

'Silas Finklebean.'

Both Freddy and Howie whipped around to look at him.

Theodore continued. 'I think Silas Finklebean went into the future and did what you're doing now. You remember what the librarian told you? That Silas was very lucky when it came to *betting* on things?'

'That's right,' admitted Freddy. 'That's what she said.'

'So what,' said Howie. 'She also said he made a lot of money.'

'And he also disappeared, Howie,' Theodore reminded him.

Howie paled. 'Oh, boy, he did, didn't he?'

'Silas Finklebean,' mumbled Freddy distractedly as he looked at his screen. Suddenly the screen changed and they were staring at a picture of Silas Finklebean with all the information from the computer's database, including his current address in Pookesville.

'My gosh,' said Freddy after they'd finished reading. 'Silas Finklebean is right here.' He jumped up. 'Come on, guys!'

CHAPTER 22

BUSTING OUT THE BEAN

Freddy knocked on the apartment door on the top floor of the tallest building in Pookesville. As he listened to the footsteps coming towards the door, his heart started to pound faster and faster: He would finally be meeting Silas Finklebean, the only person who'd ever figured out how to travel through time.

When Silas Finklebean opened the door, Freddy and the others realized that they'd all been holding their breaths. Now they let it all out with a collective *whoosh*. As Freddy stared up at the very tall man, he noticed that Finklebean appeared to be wearing the same clothes he had on from the picture in the book.

Finklebean's first words were very surprising. 'Come in, come in, I was expecting you.' He shook all of their hands as he led them inside and motioned them into chairs. The apartment, Freddy noticed, didn't look modern at all. In one corner stood an old-fashioned radio. On the wall across from Freddy was an antique clock with a long brass pendulum. Hanging on another wall was an old mercury barometer.

'I like to keep things from my own time around,' explained Finklebean.

'It's an honour to meet you, Mr Finklebean,' said Freddy.

'Well, it's an honour to meet you, Freddy,' replied Finklebean.

Howie's eyes nearly fell out of his face. 'How'd you know his name?'

'Your present is my history, so of course I know all about you.'

'So you came into the future and stayed because you wanted to?' said Freddy.

Finklebean smiled sadly. 'Well, that's not exactly what happened.'

'Indeed, if you had liked the future so much you wouldn't have surrounded yourself with the past in your apartment,' deduced Theodore.

Finklebean sighed and sat back. 'The future has its good points, but being out of your own time isn't exactly all it's cracked up to be.' He sud-denly sat forward and said very earnestly. 'That's why I wanted you to come and help me.'

'*You* wanted *us* to come?' exclaimed Freddy.

Finklebean nodded. 'I didn't know what else to do. I was desperate to get out of the future. I just don't fit in here.'

'So why couldn't you just go back in your own time machine?' asked Howie.

'It's not that simple,' replied Finklebean. 'I need your help to do that.'

'Before we can help you, we want to know everything,' said Freddy very firmly.

'You're certainly entitled to an explanation,' Finklebean acknowledged. 'Well, my story is quite simple. None of my inventions made any money. And then I invented the time travel machine and started travelling through time. It was a lot of fun at first. I had all these ideas of the good I could do for people. To go into the future and get the cures for diseases and bring them back. And to build inventions to help people, like for solar power and growing crops more efficiently, things like that. But the only person I really ended up helping was myself.'

Theodore and Freddy exchanged glances. Freddy looked a little ashamed.

Theodore said to Finklebean, 'What you *did* was make money by betting on things, because you already knew the winners.'

'It's true,' admitted Finklebean. 'I got greedy. The thing is, the more money I made the more I wanted.'

'What happened after that?' asked Theodore.

'I came into the future once too often. The Pookesville Robotic Police discovered what I was doing and they took my time machine away. You see, lots of people have time machines nowadays. And so they made it a law that prohibits using information from the future to profit in the past. I broke that law and I've been stuck here ever since.'

'But you disappeared a long time ago,' said Howie. 'And you haven't aged.'

'That's one thing I discovered when time travelling. If you're not in your own time, time essentially stands still for you.'

'So you mean you're, like, never going to die?' asked Meese.

'That's pretty darn cool, if you ask me,' added Si.

'It's not really cool if you don't have anyone who cares about you,' explained Silas. 'All my family and friends are long gone. I simply don't belong here.' He stared at them. 'What I would really like to do is go home, to my own time. Will you help me?'

Freddy looked at him oddly. 'Wait a minute. I saw you in the basement of the Burger Castle and you were floating in air. That got us curious, and then we found the logbook with the plans for the time machine in there. Can you explain that?'

Finklebean looked embarrassed. 'Can we put it down to an amazing coincidence?'

'I think not,' said Theodore, his eyes spinning rapidly. 'I calculate the odds of such a coincidence to be 4,893,987,634 to one.'

'Boy, even *I'm* not that lucky,' said Si.

'Spill the beans, Finkle*bean*!' cried Howie, 'or we leave you here to rot.'

'Well, all right.' He led them to a machine over in the corner of the room. 'Even though they took my time machine away, I still have the benefit of today's technology. This is a quantum unimolecular imaging time-warp transponder with holographic capability. I call it QUIT for short.'

'Hey, I know that word,' said Wally.

'Yeah, as in you never *quit* eating,' said Ziggy.

'It allowed me to send my holographic image back in time. I saw you in the basement that night. I had read of you and your father's accomplishments as inventors in the history books. I knew that of all the people who had access to my lab in the castle since I'd left, you or your father were the only ones capable of building the time machine from my plans. So I tried to help you along the way.'

'Wait a minute. My dad and I are in the history books?' asked Freddy. 'WOW!'

'That's right. It might have been easier for us if I'd been able to talk through the QUIT, but I'm not sure that part of the device works.'

'I think most people thought you were a ghost and ran away. That's what we did at first. And all that came out of your mouth was a long moan,' said Freddy. 'At some point one of the owners of the Burger Castle must have walled up the passageway to your lab. We only found it accidentally. We also discovered a corridor going across the street and a trapdoor into another building.'

Finklebean nodded. 'I owned another place across the street. It was a huge playhouse for the town's children. I thought it would be neat to also have a spooky corridor and trapdoor for kids to explore.'

Theodore said, 'The Patty Cakes restaurant must have been built on top of it.'

Freddy exclaimed, 'But that still doesn't explain how we ended up in the exact year where you are!'

Finklebean just shook his head. 'I don't really know. As I said, I've tried to use the device to communicate with people over the years, but I guess I just scared them away. One time I thought I had actually contacted my family and let them know what year I was in, but I don't know if they got the message or not. I guess your coming to this year must have been a coincidence after all.'

'Hmm, I wonder,' said Freddy.

'I miss my family,' said Finklebean sadly. 'I never got to see my daughter grow up. All the money and fame in the world can't make up for that.'

'Well,' said Freddy. 'It looks like you've learned your lesson.'

Finklebean clapped his hands together. 'You mean you'll do it? You'll take me home?'

Freddy looked at his gang. 'What do you think?'

'I say we bust the bean out of the future!' shouted Wally. 'And put him back where he belongs.'

'YEAH!' shouted Howie.

'Isecondthatmotionandvoteayetoo,' mumbled Curly.

'Ditto to what Curly said – although I have no idea what it was,' said Si.

'OK,' added Meese miserably, 'although I'm probably going to live to regret it. Or more likely *die*.'

'Let's go,' squeaked Ziggy.

Freddy looked at Theodore. 'Theodore, what do you think?'

The blue Fry cleared his throat and said, 'I think everyone has learned a valuable lesson about the perils of using time for their own personal gain. And I think we should *all* go back to where we came from.'

Freddy looked at Theodore and smiled. 'You really are one smart Fry.'

'Now it won't be easy,' said Finklebean quickly. 'I mean, I broke the law, and while I'm not in jail or anything, I am prohibited from using a time travel machine for any reason.' He pointed to a device on his wrist. 'This allows them to follow my every move. The Robotic Police are very smart.'

'No problem,' said Si confidently. 'They haven't run into this gang before.'

Finklebean looked at the Fries one by one. 'Excuse me for asking, but what exactly are you?'

'Aluminum coiled, carbon-tubed, microchip-powered with just a touch of the finest Idaho potato,' replied Theodore.

'In other words, we are kick-butt spuds,' bellowed Wally.

Freddy thought for a bit and then said, 'OK, this actually should be pretty easy. The police can't know about our time machine because it's invisible. It's on the other side of Pookesville, near the town square.' Freddy described the exact location for Silas. 'You leave a few minutes after us and head there too, only by a different route. We'll jump in the time machine and be long gone before anyone even knows.'

'Sounds like a plan, Freddio,' said Si.

'Well, just be careful,' warned Finklebean. 'I've tried to escape before and the police have always caught me. And since you're helping me, they'll arrest you too.'

'We'll take that chance,' said Freddy confidently.

Freddy and the gang left the apartment and headed to the time machine. Finklebean left a few minutes later. However, twenty feet behind Finklebean, something was following him.

When Freddy and the gang reached the time machine, Freddy hit the button turning off the invisibility shield. He checked his watch. 'OK, Finklebean will be here any minute. Let's get in the time machine and be ready to take off.'

A minute later Ziggy squeaked, 'There he is.'

'Right on time,' said Si. 'I love it when a plan comes together.'

'OR NOT!' yelled Meese. 'Look!' He pointed right behind Finklebean.

A dozen robotic policemen were charging towards them.

'Mr Finklebean, look out,' yelled Freddy.

'You look out too,' shouted Finklebean, pointing behind Freddy.

The gang whirled around and saw police robots coming from all directions.

'I told you they were very smart,' shouted Finklebean.

'Evasive action, guys,' ordered Freddy.

The police quickly grabbed Finklebean, but Freddy, Howie and the Fries started scrambling. Big Wally was gone like a shot, a purple blur that disappeared around some buildings.

A squadron of robots suddenly zoomed into the

air. 'Oh, great, they can fly!' said Freddy as the robots swooped down at them.

'What's the big deal? So can we,' said Si. He and Meese held their breaths and floated into the air. One robot ran into them in midair and dropped to the ground.

Curly uncoiled to his full height, grabbed hold of two robots and was pulled into the air. He held on tight and when they passed close to a building, Curly reached out and grabbed onto a flagpole. This brought both robots up short. Curly reeled them in and then tied them to the flagpole using the flag as a rope. Then he dropped to the ground.

'BoythatwasfunbutIdon'twanttodoitagain,' he said, panting.

Two of the robots were zooming right at Ziggy. An instant before they got to him he hit himself on the back of the head and fell apart. The two robots collided with each other and fell to the ground.

Theodore was confronted by another robot. 'You must surrender at once in accordance with Pookesville Penal Code section 103.456-63.'

Theodore thought quickly. 'Yes, but under the United States Constitution, I'm allowed one phone call to my lawyer. Can you go and find one for me, please?'

'Absolutely, sir, I'll be right back.' As soon as the robot left Theodore scampered away.

Meanwhile, Howie and Freddy were cornered by three robots.

'You must surrender,' said one of them. 'It is against the law to aid a prisoner to escape.'

'Never! We'll fight to the death,' declared Howie.

Freddy grabbed Howie by the shirt. 'Will you shut up before you get us killed?'

Freddy turned back to the robots. 'This is all a misunderstanding. We're not even from this time.'

'We know,' said one of the robots. 'You came here to learn about the future so you can profit from it in your own time, just like Silas Finklebean did.'

'He's got us there, Freddy,' said Howie. 'We're guilty, guilty, guilty!'

'Will you keep quiet, Howie,' said an exasperated Freddy. 'OK, guys, I think after I explain what happened, everything will be cool. See, I'm Freddy and I'm an inventor. And . . .'

One of the robots pulled out what looked like a crossbow and fired. A big net sailed up and then started to fall on top of the boys.

'I don't think they're buying your explanation, Freddy,' said Howie.

Right before the net closed over them it was yanked away. They watched as Curly rose over them, the net in hand. He threw it over the two robots and they dropped to the ground.

'Gee, thanks, Curly,' said Freddy.

'Noproblemgladtodoitbutwe'restillinalotof-trouble,' mumbled Curly.

'What did he say?' asked Howie.

'You don't want to know,' answered Freddy.

Freddy and the gang were surrounded now and the robots were closing in.

'I'm sorry, Freddy,' said Finklebean. 'I should never have gotten you into this.'

'It's OK, Mr Finklebean,' said Freddy. 'It wasn't your fault. It was mine. I should have left time

travel alone.' He turned to Howie. 'If these guys lock us up we'll never see our families again. Heck, I can't believe I'm saying this, but I'll even miss my nutty sister.'

The robots readied to fire nets over all of them when they heard the voice.

'This looks like a job for PURPULIS ENORMOSIS!'

They turned and saw Wally strolling up to one of the robots. 'Have you got any of those little food thingie-wingie, pillsies-willsies?' he asked. 'You know, to give a condemned Fry his last meal?'

The robots pulled a bunch of pills out and handed them to Wally.

'Wally,' scolded Ziggy, 'this is no time to eat.'

'Little yellow papoosie, it's always a good time to eat.'

'Don't eat them all at once,' advised the robot.

Wally smiled and then swallowed every last one of them. 'Take cover, guys,' yelled Wally. 'This is gonna be purpulis enormosis like you've never seen him.'

Freddy, Silas Finklebean and the other Fries dropped to the ground.

'YYYEEEAAAHHH!' One pill had made Wally grow two feet in the gut. Now, with a handful of pills, he was busting out twelve feet in all directions.

Next he started twirling around on his tiptoes like a top, and his enormous body mowed down every single robotic policeman in sight. Then he let out a huge burp and returned to normal size.

'Purpulis enormosis, you rule!' cried Howie.

They all raced to the time machine and climbed in. As soon as Finklebean set the time dial, Freddy hit GO.

The time machine blasted off at the speed of light, and flashes of colour streaked past the windows. A minute later the time machine slid to a stop. Freddy opened the hatch and they were all staring at the Burger Castle. Well, it wasn't the Burger Castle now; it was Castle Finklebean.

Freddy said, 'Mr Finklebean, if you could invent a time travel machine, you can invent lots of useful inventions that'll work right here in your own time. So forget the curvy car and the candy bar and focus on something really useful.'

'Hey, that candy bar was really cool!' exclaimed Wally indignantly. 'And I should know since I personally ate 1,165 of them.'

Finklebean patted Freddy on the shoulder. 'You're right, Freddy.'

Finklebean climbed out and now there were tears in his eyes as he looked at his home. He turned back to Freddy. 'I can't thank you enough for everything.'

A little girl ran out from the Castle. 'Daddy!' she cried.

Finklebean lifted her up and gave her a kiss.

'I missed you so much, Daddy.'

'I missed you too, honey.'

Freddy looked at the little girl and said to himself, 'I was right. The picture on the mantel.'

Freddy and the gang waved good-bye to the Finklebeans.

'Let's go home, guys,' said Freddy as the hatch closed and he hit the GO button.

CHAPTER 23

ALL'S WELL THAT ENDS FUNKY

Adam was still screaming foul. And Nancy had single-handedly beaten up the Spanker gang using her baton, a fire extinguisher and lots of dialogue from Shakespeare. And the purple goop-covered Stewie Spanker was still trying to wash himself off in the Burger Castle moat. That's when the time machine reappeared.

Freddy opened the hatch and they climbed out. Everyone crowded around them.

'Where did you *go*?' asked a reporter from the *Pookesville Tattler*.

'We travelled into the future,' said Howie.

The crowd laughed.

'Do you have proof of that?' asked one of the judges.

'Sure, we can tell you everything that we –' began Howie, but Freddy quickly kicked him in the shin.

Freddy said, 'No, we don't have any proof, sir.'

Stewie Spanker climbed out of the moat and

came waddling up. 'You ruined the Patty Cakes restaurant and I'm gonna sue you for that.'

'I didn't!' said Freddy. 'Adam aimed it at the *Burger Castle*. You two planned it.'

'How can you accuse us of something dirty like that?' exclaimed Stewie Spanker. 'I'm the mayor and the chief of police and a darn nice guy.' Then he roared, 'So after we take every dime you have, I'm going to string you up by your thumbs and make you drink every last drop of that purple junk, you little jerk!'

'You had it aimed at the Burger Castle,' insisted Freddy. 'All I did was move the directional control so it would shoot straight up.'

'That's a lie, because it didn't shoot straight up!' roared Stewie.

'Then someone else must have changed it after I did. I bet it was Adam.'

'A likely story,' sneered Stewie.

'Yeah, that's right,' said Adam. 'Harold Pumpernickel did all the work. I've never even been on that stupid volcano.'

'Yes, he has,' said a voice. 'And I can prove it.'

All heads turned. There was Harold Pumpernickel holding a video camera.

'What?' asked an astonished Freddy.

'I filmed it with my spy camera,' said Harold. 'Here, see for yourselves.'

He turned on the video camera and they all

watched as Adam snuck in the volcano mouth and aimed the directional control.

'Only instead of moving the control clockwise so it would hit the Burger Castle,' said Harold, 'Adam moved it *counter*clockwise so it hit the Patty Cakes.'

'I know what clockwise means, you little moron,' yelled Adam. 'It means to the *left*. AND THAT'S THE WAY I TURNED IT.'

'Actually,' said Alfred Funkhouser, 'clockwise means to the *right*.'

Adam's eyes bugged out and he swallowed hard. 'Whoops!'

Stewie looked at his son. 'Adam, I'm ashamed of you. Why, I can't imagine a son of mine doing something so underhanded and dirty. As punishment you get no more chocolate tornado milkshakes for a whole hour.'

'But, Dad! You were the one—'

'Not another word,' roared his father as he stalked off, still covered in purple goop.

The judges had all been huddled together while this was going on. Then one of them stepped forward. 'We don't exactly know where Freddy disappeared to, and he has no proof that he went into the future, so in the interests of fairness we can't give the prize to him. And since Adam Spanker just admitted that Harold did all of the work on that fabulous volcano, he's out too. So we've decided to declare Harold Pumpernickel, who *did* do all the work, the winner of the science competition.'

The crowd cheered and Freddy clapped louder than anyone as Harold received the trophy and check for a hundred dollars. Harold's father put his son on his shoulders and paraded around.

Alfred came over to Freddy and put his arm around him. 'Well, Freddy, how *was* the future?'

Freddy gulped as he stared at his father. But his father was the smartest person Freddy knew. As absentminded as he appeared at times, Alfred Funkhouser seemed to know *everything*.

'Let's put it this way, Dad. Travelling into the past and future sounds cool, but it's a lot smarter to stay in your *own* time.'

As Alfred Funkhouser left to congratulate Harold, Mildred Maraschino came up to Freddy.

'Oh, Freddy,' said Mildred, 'I can't thank you enough.'

'For what, Ms Maraschino?'

'For bringing Silas back.' She handed him a book. It was a copy of *The Entire History of Pookesville in 31 1/2 Pages*. It was open to a particular page. Freddy read it quickly.

'It doesn't say here that Silas Finklebean disappeared! It just says that he was a very successful inventor and a great father.' He paused and said, 'He was your father, wasn't he?'

She looked surprised. 'Yes, he was my father.

Before my marriage my name was Mildred Finklebean. How did you know?'

'When we went to your cottage I saw a picture on your mantel of two people. One looked a lot like you as a young girl and the other looked like Silas Finklebean. That's why I thought he might have left the gyroscope with you. And the little girl who ran out to see him when we brought Silas back to his time *was* the little girl in that photo, meaning you.'

She smiled kindly at him. 'You *are* one smart young man.'

'I saw you over near the time machine before we went into the future. Were you the one who set the time dial to 2206?'

She nodded. 'When I was a little girl I thought I heard my father talking to me. He said the number 2206 over and over. I thought I was dreaming.'

'He was sending you a message from the future using the QUIT.' Mildred looked puzzled and Freddy quickly added, 'It's sort of complicated.'

'Well, I never told anyone because they would have thought I was crazy. But when I saw your time machine today I recognized it from some plans that I saw in my father's lab. I knew he was working on some sort of time travel thing, and it struck me that the number *2206* might actually be the *year* where he was. So I snuck into the machine and set the time dial. I could only hope that it would take you to him.'

'Well, that clears that up,' Freddy said, but then he looked puzzled. 'But since we changed the past, the 'future' never happened in the way it did before. So how did you even know about us?'

'Easy. Silas told me when he got back. Just like you remembered what happened.'

'Well, I guess that's the mystery of time travel that we'll never completely understand.'

Mildred took something out of her pocketbook and handed it to him. It was the 'wishing' mirror her father had given her. 'I wanted you to have this, seeing as how you helped make my wish of having my father back come true.' She gave him a hug and then left.

As Freddy watched her go, he heard a scream behind him. Storming out of the Burger Castle was his sister Nancy. She was covered in paint and carrying what looked to be pieces of torn canvas. Behind her came a photographer and reporter from the *Pookesville Tattler*, laughing their heads off.

'Freddy Funkhouser, I am going to cream you, you little rat,' she screamed.

'What did I do?'

'You know very well what you did, or should I say, *didn't* do. The Nancy S. Funkhouser Imperial Theatre and Museum? There's nothing there, you little jerk!'

Freddy looked at Si. 'What did you do?'

'Hee-hee,' laughed Si nervously. 'It's sort of a long, depressing story and I'm just too happy a Fry to tell it.'

'I told you,' moaned a terrified Meese as he watched Nancy stomping towards them. 'She's going to massacre all of us.'

'Not me she's not,' yelled Si. 'See you in the future.' He and Meese took off running towards the time machine with the others in hot pursuit.

'Stop!' said Freddy. He, Howie and the other Fries raced after them with Nancy right behind. But Wally, who was just inches ahead of Nancy, couldn't stop in time. He slammed into the gang and they all sailed headfirst into the time machine and the hatch slammed shut behind them. Nancy pounded on the hatch futilely. 'Come out of there, you creep, so I can annihilate you!'

Wally was right next to the control panel.

'Whatever you do, Wally, *don't* hit the GO button,' warned Freddy, who was squashed in the back.

'What, this one?' said Wally as he pushed the button.

'WWWAAALLLYYY!' they all screamed to-gether as the time machine blasted off once more.